DS 10/10

AS 6/13

TC 6.12 | BC 3.15

RE

Please return/renew this item by the last date shown

worcestershire
countycouncil
Cultural Services

HIGH LAWLESS

HIGH LAWLESS

A Western Story

T. V. OLSEN

SAGEBRUSH
Large Print Westerns

First published in Great Britain by Muller
First published in the United States by Fawcett Gold Medal

Published in Large Print 2010 by ISIS Publishing Ltd.,
7 Centremead, Osney Mead, Oxford OX2 0ES
United Kingdom
by arrangement with
Golden West Literary Agency

British Library Cataloguing in Publication Data
Olsen, Theodore V.
    High lawless.
    1. Western stories.
    2. Large type books.
    I. Title
    813.5'4–dc22

ISBN 978–0–7531–8518–6 (hb)

Printed and bound in Great Britain by
T. J. International Ltd., Padstow, Cornwall

CHAPTER
ONE

He stepped from his saddle at the tie rail, wrapped his reins around the weathered crosspole, and had his look at the nearly deserted, noon-slumbering main street. Los Santos was a primitive Mexican-American village nestled in an upper crook of the Rio Grande. The buildings, monotonously white-washed adobe paralleled by dirt paths, were afforded a single rickety relief in the raw, unpainted frame structure of Ranson's saloon. Beyond it and etched against the brassy sky above it, a church flaunted an ironic spire.

With no waste motion he lifted his carbine from its scabbard, pivoted on his heel and headed down the street for the saloon. Picked out in the midday sun, he was compact, not hard, with the relaxed alertness of a cat. His calico shirt and waist overalls were threadbare, worn to a neutral chalk-gray where alkali had not obscured their color. His eyes were brittle amber, without looking to left or right they missed nothing, and the angular surface lines of his face warned a man that he rarely smiled. In his mid-twenties, not quite a small man, he carried himself with a quiet, not-cocky yet uncompromising confidence that usually only bigger and older men could afford. Something, not in

1

his face but in his fluid movements, suggested a sum of thin temper on the edge of violence; a Mexican woman coming from the plaza well with a water *olla* on her shoulder angled discreetly away from his path.

Walking on a long angle, he reached the opposite side of the street where a small adobe store adjoined the saloon, and paused there. Pop Killaine was slacked massively in his back-tilted chair against the store front. Pop was fat, bald and seventy, a local patriarch; he was to be seen here every day, rain or shine, watching the small currents of life that made Los Santos a town — seeing much, saying little. Hooded beneath frosty brows, his eyes probed at the rifle, then lifted to the young man's face.

"Primed for bear?"

"You saw him, Pop." It was a statement, not a question.

"Next door. Buckin' the tiger, drinking up a storm."

"I reckoned he was."

Pop Killaine paused weightily, clearing his throat. "He's with Costello."

"I guessed that, too." The young man's tone was bitter and musing. "What's got into him, Pop?"

"Whiskey, Channing."

Channing nodded once before making an abrupt half-turn and heading on to Ranson's. He shouldered the swing doors open and went through.

The barroom was overhung with stale whiskey fumes and a thinly curling stratum of cigar smoke; at the long bar cowboys rubbed shoulders with feed-lot men, stock buyers, and drummers, for it was shipping time and the

2

saloons of the sleepy village were the center of commerce for this remote corner of the territory. An archway draped with beaded curtains joined the barroom and the gambling hall at the back, and the whir of roulette wheel and keno goose mingled with the murmurs or explosive laughter of many men.

Channing crossed the barroom and pushed aside the beaded curtains. The gambling tables were all crowded, but he thought he glimpsed Lacey's blond head at the back of the room. He moved that way, threading between tables.

A lean body shifted casually across his path, blocking him. He halted, facing Bee Withers. Withers was a foolish, untalkative man of forty in filthy denims. Costello's man. He cheeked a tobacco cud in one whiskered jaw and spat cheerfully at the floor between them.

"Want to buy in?" Channing asked.

Not moving, Withers said nothing, grinning vacuously because he knew that Channing could be crowded a long way.

"Don't," Channing said quietly, just watching. Withers' grin faded as he realized that Channing already considered himself pushed to a limit. He let out his breath slowly, almost delicately, and stepped carefully to one side. Channing moved on without a sideward glance and halted at Costello's table.

Lacey Trobridge's head was hunched between his heavy shoulders as he squinted befuddledly at a fan of cards in his meaty fist. He did not look up. The dealer did, his bland, dark gambler's eyes raising to

Channing's. He was a slight, almost ash-blond man in fawn-colored trousers and a bottle-green frock coat. There was a faint, autocratic arrogance about Ward Costello that went beyond dapper airs.

"Lacey," Channing said now, gently.

Lacey raised his head, tossing his blond cowlick out of his eyes. They were a wide, innocuous china-blue, the kind that went quick with pain at the sight of a motherless calf or a saddle-galled horse. His eyes usually held an eager, wagging-tailed friendliness that instantly won both men and women — and masked a score of faults and weaknesses that Channing knew and forgave. Just now the eyes were slitted and bloodshot in Lacey's red face. He recognized Channing, muttered surlily, "Knew you'd be here," and reached for the glass at his elbow.

Channing nudged the glass with the tip of his rifle-barrel; it shattered on the floor in a dark reeking splash. Lacey's hand froze in arrested movement; behind Channing, the room died into silence.

Lacey tried to dredge up anger, failed, and said plaintively, "No need for that, boy. I'm free, white —"

"And drunk," Channing said. "Do you leave on your own feet or feet first?"

"I'd go easy, Channing," Costello murmured.

"Why?"

They stared at each other for a time-hung space which Costello broke: "Take him when the game's over, then."

"I'll take him now."

4

"Damn it," Lacey slurred, "don't talk about me like I wasn't here!"

"Shut up," Channing said. "Get on your feet." As he spoke he shifted his rifle to his left hand, caught Lacey under the arm and started to lift him from the chair. The brief side-flick of Costello's eyes was enough to warn Channing; he let go of Lacey and wheeled, swung up his rifle and smashed the stock savagely against Bee Withers' down-arcing forearm. Withers shouted with pain, the six-gun he'd swung at Channing's temple falling from nerveless fingers. Without a break in movement, Channing swung his rifle back and forward, the barrel meeting Withers' jaw in a merciless, cracking blow. Withers' legs dissolved; without a sound he slumped to the floor.

"Ed — behind you —"

Lacey's cry brought Channing around, facing back to the table. There was no law in Los Santos; by tacit consent its tough-nut inhabitants settled their disputes personally and a single blunt warning, if that, was as much as a man could expect. He barely caught a single flicking motion of Costello's hand; a pocket pistol appeared in that hand as by magic.

If Costello had meant only to bluff, there was no time now; Channing's rifle was coming to level, and Costello fired as Lacey Trobridge's straining lunge carried him across the table between them. Lacey jerked heavily with the slug's impact; his body plunged aspraddle the table and slid off as it crashed on its side. Cards and chips rained over his inert form.

Costello was already running, heading toward a rear door. Channing, shaking with rage, straightened from the body of his friend. He brought the carbine to his shoulder, tried to bead down on the gambler. But every man in the room was on his feet now; a press of shifting bodies cut off Channing's view. The door swung wide; Costello bolted through and slammed it behind him. Channing elbowed through the crowd to achieve the door. Trying to force it, he saw through a quarter-inch crack that a heavy crossbar had been dropped into brackets.

He flung about and elbowed through the curtained archway into the barroom. Men cursed him as they gave way. He ran the length of the room and the swing doors parted with his hurtling body. He veered hard, skirted the building and pounded up the adjoining alley past the startled Pop Killaine. He found Costello's running footprints deep-dug in the soft earth at the rear of the building. The gambler had cut hard to the right, his steps fading out then on the hard turf.

Channing went down on one knee, tracing the back-springing grass bent by Costello's flight. *You'll find him, the town isn't that big it'll hide him long,* he considered with an icy detachment, and then: *The stable. He'll try to clear out.*

At once he was on his feet, paralleling the rear of the buildings at a plunging run. The livery stable was at street's end, a long, high structure backed by a horse corral. The horses were milling skittishly; between their bodies he saw Costello appear in the livery's rear archway and glance swiftly around. The gambler abruptly pivoted in midstride; Channing caught the sunflash on the pocket pistol, again magically palmed. He dived through the corral poles, lit on his side as the little gun made its spiteful bark; shards of wood bit from a fence pole. Rolling now to his feet, he thought automatically, *That's both barrels.*

The snorting horses leaped away as he lunged across the compound. He reached the archway and hauled up short. In the center of the runway the gray-haired hostler was holding a horse; Costello had a toe in stirrup. His face, pinched with fear, swung toward Channing; he hesitated and then vaulted into leather. Channing lowered his rifle, then hefted it with both hands around the stock as he started forward.

"Come off there or I'll knock you off."

Costello had not spurred away, for Channing could have easily shot him from the saddle. Now, seeing Channing's revised intent, he snatched the reins from the hostler and roweled the animal savagely, driving it squarely at Channing.

Channing swung the rifle back, intending to leap aside and sweep Costello from his perch with a full-arm swing. As he moved his boot skidded on the wet clay of the runway; he flailed his arms, fighting for balance, and then the horse's shoulder smashed him full in the chest. The impact drove the breath from him. His last-ditch effort to keep his footing had arched his body backward and now he plunged helplessly to one side, felt a crashing blow on his skull, and then awareness pinwheeled away into darkness.

He came to with the hostler gently slapping his face with the end of a wet rag. He pushed the old man's hand away. Pain rocked sickeningly in his head as he fought to a sitting position, then cradled his face in his palms. When the dizziness had receded he looked up.

"Costello?"

"Hypered out like the Old Nick was scorching his heels. Evil lick, that. Crown of your hat blunted it or you'd a took a split head, more'n likely . . . ."

Channing turned his head to see the heavy corner post of the stall partition which he had fallen against. With the old man's shoulder for support he got to his feet, swallowed against a roiling sickness, and made his voice steady. "Take my hat, old-timer."

The hostler picked up the mashed Stetson, batted the crown to rough shape and silently handed it to him. Channing adjusted it well forward on his throbbing head, nodded thanks, and walked gingerly from the stable, halting at the front archway.

The gray taste of defeat was in his mouth. Careless overcertainty had permitted the gambler's escape. It would take time, trailing him in the stony hills above town, and meanwhile Costello would put miles between himself and Los Santos. There had to be one sure way to find him, and then Channing had the answer. It quickened his pace as he walked back to Ranson's.

In the gambling room he found a sober crowd gathered around Lacey's body, spread over now by a worn blanket. Bee Withers was propped unconscious and spraddle-legged against the wall and Dr. Alverez, the ancient settlement medico, was kneeling by him and tentatively probing at his jaw with long, bony fingers.

"How is he?" Channing asked.

Alverez looked up and said in his reedy and trembling voice, "You are the young *ladrone* who did this?"

"*Replicar,*" Channing said coldly, sharply.

Alverez sighed with a vague shrug. "The lower mandibular is shattered. It will have to be wired up for a long time. I do not know who will pay. It will be very painful."

Bueno, Channing thought, and aloud: "*¿Cuànto es?*"

The medico blinked his watery eyes rapidly. "Twenty dollars."

"And I'm a *ladrone?* Ten." Alverez didn't object. Channing counted out the silver dollars, clinked them into the withered palm, and walked over to Lacey. He started to reach for the blanket where it covered the boy's face, hesitated and straightened, hat in hand, staring bleakly down. His thoughts left the crowded, murmurous room. ranging back to other days, good days he and the dead boy had known together. He didn't want to see Lacey's face. *He was always so alive,* Channing thought. *Maybe too alive.* Maybe that was it . . . .

Nine months ago they had thrown in together to hunt wild mustangs in the rocky border hills. Channing had had his own reasons for wanting to temporarily abandon the society of men, and wanting to get Lacey

Trobridge away from it too. The kid was not mean-tempered but incorrigibly wild in an easy, free-swinging way; trouble usually found him before he looked for it. Channing's problem had been similar; perhaps that was why he'd been attracted to this mercurial boy whose brash, out-going temperament was at odds with his own. It had made him almost paternally protective.

The work had been hard, up in their lonely horse camp twenty miles from Los Santos, their only company the half-dozen Mexican wranglers they'd hired who hung apart from the two Americans. Brutal labor on a thin, monotonous diet of coarse *frijoles* and jerky and over-watered chicory. It meant riding out a hundred miserable vagaries of weather, breaking backs and blisters building horse-traps and driving the animals to them, rough-busting the captured mustangs, finally rolling into their blankets at day's end too exhausted for talk. Lacey had griped incessantly; only his friend's stronger personality had held him from riding off a dozen times.

It's going to be different, Channing had argued; we'll clear anyway two thousand before we're finished . . . enough for a big down payment on a little ranch north a ways I've had my eye on for a long time. No more pounding leather for thirty and found, throwing it all away on payday. Be our own men . . . and partners, eh?

Lacey had airily agreed, only half-hiding his indifference. As a token of trust Channing had him drive the first bunch of mustangs to Los Santos to dicker a price; Lacey's friendly ways should fetch a

10

good sum, give the kid a needed sense of responsibility. A mistake. Lacey had gotten a good price . . . then headed for the nearest gambling room. Dealer Ward Costello had obligingly set up the drinks while he took Lacey for every cent. That had been three months ago.

Channing had hardly castigated the kid; the bitter truth was too plain. Lacey would never bear responsibility if he lived to a hundred: an omission in his nature that could not be filled. The most he could hope was to steer the boy — another futile hope.

Last night after patiently hearing out Lacey's usual tirade of complaints, Channing had announced that they had enough mustangs for a second sale — at least a thousand dollars' worth — and that they'd drive to Los Santos tomorrow. This morning he had rolled out of his blankets to find Lacey gone. Bleakly certain that Lacey had ridden to town to hit the tables again on the strength of his share of the mustang proceeds, he'd saddled up and told the wranglers to follow him with the horses, and then headed alone for Los Santos . . .

A hand touched his arm. He turned to face the beefy bartender. The man's tough face and voice were gruffly sympathetic. "Sorry as hell. Seen something of the sort coming."

With an effort Channing mustered speech. "There'll be a cost for —"

"Don't trouble your purse, friend; he'll be well buried as a man ever is here." Brushing aside a word of thanks, he said again, "Sorry as hell. Good friend, eh?"

Good friend, Channing's mind echoed. Just a damn fool boy who couldn't keep away from the cards and

11

the liquor and the fancy ladies — and the knowledge changed nothing. He knew how badly he had needed this one friend, and Ward Costello had killed him.

He found himself standing outside in front of Ranson's and there was Pop Killaine crossing the street with his rolling waddle, leading Channing's claybank gelding from the tie rail across the way. Wordlessly he halted, threw the reins.

"Thanks, Pop." Channing stepped to the animal's flank, sheathed the carbine. With the same deft economy of movement he untied the blanket roll behind the cantle and unrolled it He lifted out a coiled gunbelt and holster. The belt was supple and oiled, the holster-leather purposely stiff and unworked and the inside rubbed slick with tallow. The Colt's .45 it held glided from leather almost at his touch, its weight balanced easily, naturally, in his palm. He spun the cylinder; it turned as though on oiled jewel-bearings.

Pop released a gently explosive grunt. "That bad?"

Channing glanced at him, saying thinly, "Anything you miss, Pop?"

"Not a hell of a lot. Seen a lot of guntippers try to hang up iron, never worked. Don't break the mold now."

The dry sarcasm was felt in his words and not in the old man's tired tonelessness. His eyes were sad with a kindly cynicism. Channing shrugged. "With a reason, anyway."

"No. No good. Boy's dead, it can't bring him back. I'd think on it, son. Hard."

Channing drew an impatient breath, yet his hands hesitated around the belt.

"Might be you'll not need it," Pop Killaine suggested softly.

Channing leathered the gun, wrapped the belt around the holster and returned it to the blanket roll with swift, angry movements. "This won't change things."

"All right, all right, man's got to pay, see he does. But go easy . . . Seen him ride north. There's law up there. You —"

"Where would he go, Pop?"

Pop shook his head. "Costello, he drifted in, out. Had more money than most sharpers, always wore the finest, ate the best. With the airs of him I'd suspicion him of a fancy background. More'n that, can't say."

Channing nodded, turning away. Instead of mounting he started back toward the stable, leading his horse. Pop Killaine huffed into step with him. "Thought you'd be hell-for-leather."

"I'm a patient man, Pop. I can wait."

"For what?"

"I cracked Bee Withers' jaw. It'll keep him abed awhile. When he's on his feet . . . he's Costello's heel dog. He'll head for where Costello is."

"And you'll follow. Streak of Injun in you, Channing. Wager you can hate like one, too."

"No bet," Channing said unsmilingly. He halted, facing the old man. "Do me a favor. My wranglers are coming in with a horse herd. I'll be at the hotel. Sleeping on a headache. Tell 'em."

"Sure," Pop said gently. "I'll tell 'em . . ."

He stood unmoving as Channing went on toward the stable. Under his frosty brows the old man's eyes were sad and weary and pitying.

CHAPTER
TWO

Channing lay bellied at the summit of a long, grassy rise. His eyes were flinty, edged with impatience at last; a two weeks' growth of beard darkened his lower face and his clothing was filthy and sweat-crusted. He watched Bee Withers ride across the ranch yard and dismount. Two men were waiting for him on the main house porch, and he recognized the angular grace in the walk of the one who came down to greet Withers . . . it was Costello. They shook hands, then entered the house.

Channing rose to a crouch, easing his cramped muscles. His hard face did not reveal the cold surge of satisfaction he felt.

In Los Santos he had waited a week till Withers' broken jaw had mended enough to let him ride. During that time Channing had sold his horses and paid off his wranglers, bought a light grubstake of staples to fill his saddlebags — and waited. He'd stayed successfully out of Withers' sight, yet keeping a weather eye on his movements; when Withers had ridden from Los Santos it was openly and in broad daylight. Channing had followed, holding his measured distance. Withers had headed north, traveling fast and light. When he camped in the open Channing made dry camp close by. When he stayed in a town, Channing camped outside and was waiting each morning to pick up the trail. Withers made a few clumsy efforts to hide his sign, doubling back, making sharp cut-offs from traveled routes, but these gave Channing no difficulty. Withers was never certain he was being closely followed.

Yesterday they had entered the broad basin of the Soledad River in a northeastern pocket of New Mexico. It was mountainous, irregular country, and Channing had begun to worry whether he could hold the trail much longer. Withers had spent the night in Sentinel, a little ranch-center village situated at a bend of the river, and this morning had headed due west from town along a wagon road. At midday Withers rode into the ranch quarters below the rise where Channing now crouched.

Trail's end. Channing came stiffly to his feet and trotted halfway downslope to his claybank, ground-haltered behind the rise. Weeks of frugal meals and lack of sleep, his filthy and unkempt state, combined to hone temper to a tense edge. He mounted and rode to the crest of the rise, forcing himself to think coolly. He took in the ranch layout, missing no detail. The headquarters sprawled impressively in a rolling swale. The main house was solidly heavy-timbered and set off from the working part of the ranch. Costello was down there . . . no doubt with friends. Friends who would shield a murderer? He didn't know; ignorance gave him pause. To ride in boldly and openly might well place his head in a noose, and yet there was no choice . . .

He circled the slope, riding up behind the maze of corrals and sheds while keeping these between himself and the combination cookshack-bunkhouse on the west side of the layout. The bulk of the crew must be on-range now, at past noon; he hoped to reach the house without being seen. He put the claybank across an open space, rode up between the stables and carriage shed close to the house and then kneed his mount briskly across the scuffed, hard-packed clay yard to the porch.

He started to swing down, one foot leaving stirrup as the door opened. A middle-aged man wearing a white linen suit and a wide-brimmed Panama hat came out, walked leisurely to the porch edge. Channing finished his dismount and wrapped his reins around the long tie rail. He moved back from the rail to his horse, his scabbarded rifle within easy reach as Costello and Withers edged warily onto the porch behind the older man.

"That's him," Costello said, his low-pitched voice failing to cover its faint tremor.

The older man didn't even glance at him. Watching Channing, he drew gently on the long, thin Havana he held — an arrogant cock of wrist to the way he held it. He was small and whiplash-lean, wearing his white tropicals with a dapper elegance that seemed out of place even in a gentleman rancher. Impressive, yet foppish, till you saw his face. The eyes were pale and colorless, with an icy opaqueness that hid all emotion. The closely schooled set of his face was fine and aquiline. But his thin, incisive lips were bloodless, bracketed with severe lines, and Channing knew that this was a man who bent other men with an iron hand and was bent by no one.

He exhaled a stream of smoke into the sunlight. His tone was easy, conversational, yet with a toneless inflection that betrayed neither condescension nor hostility: his words said it bluntly. "I know who you are, why you're here, horseherd. I don't underestimate the guts, even the sagacity, of a man who would come this far for your reason. Still, you're a fool."

"I'm listening," Channing said sparely, "but not long."

The man's little finger flicked ash from the Havana. "I'm Santee Dyker. The name means a good deal around here. I can make or break any man who works for me and a lot who don't. Ward, here, is my nephew." His lips twisted faintly, cynically. "A sorry admission, but the truth. He's worth nothing, but I made a promise to his dying mother — my sister. His interests have to be mine."

"That's too bad."

"For you," Santee Dyker murmured. "Ward gave me a story that put the right on his side, which, knowing Ward, I didn't for an instant believe. Your claim doubtless has justice, but I'll not pretend a hypocritical interest in justice. Meanwhile, the killing took place far to the south; you have no friends here. As a man shrewd enough to assess the drift . . . you'd better get back on that horse."

Channing moved — an unbroken movement that lifted his rifle from the saddle, levered it and brought it to bear on the three men inclusively.

18

Dyker's relaxed pose did not alter. "Take him with you and my men will overtake you . . . Shoot him now and you won't get out of the country alive. My country." He paused with a weighted emphasis. "Hopeless, you see?"

Detachedly Channing noted the resemblance between Santee Dyker and Costello: the difference important to him was that Dyker was as strong as his nephew was weak, and Channing knew that no single word was bluff. He faced more than he had bargained for, yet the inflexible stubbornness that was part of him would not let him consider flinching down, he had come too far . . .

"Step down here, Costello. Keep your hands out from your body."

"Santee," Costello said in a choked whisper.

"Never argue with a desperate man," Dyker said smoothly. "Do as he tells you, Ward; doubt he'll shoot in cold blood, unless you resist. Nor will he get far."

Costello took two halting steps.

"Ease down that squirrel iron, boy. There's two guns covering you." The voice was deep-South, summer-soft. Channing moved only his eyes till he saw a man just coming to view from behind one corner of the house. A second man appeared at the opposite corner. Channing lowered the rifle. The two circled the porch, six-guns steady; the man who'd spoken stopped a careful yard off from Channing and took the rifle from his hands.

"Well-timed, Streak," Santee said.

Streak grinned faintly. He was a slender man of about thirty, not tall; hard and disillusioned eyes still found room for a bright, wicked arrogance in their pale-bleached depths. He leaned Channing's rifle against the porch, jerked off his dusty hat and batted it idly against his brush chaps. A streak of pure white waved back through his wiry chestnut hair. "Yeah. We'd come off fencing, was in the bunkhouse. Saw him crossing between the corrals and the carriage shed. Looked to be prowling, so we circled, come up back of the house . . . He the one you wanted us to look out for?"

"The one." Dyker stubbed out his cigar on the porch railing, colorless eyes fixing Channing. "Won't warn off, will you, horseherd? Have to be shown my meaning . . . Get a rope, Whitey."

The other man holding a gun on Channing giggled. He was twenty or less, rail-thin, with hair so pale it was nearly white. His eyes were slits. A feverish pleasure filled them. "Right away, Mr. Dyker." He loped away, vanishing behind a shed.

Streak drawled expressionlessly, "Sure this is the way?"

"Let him off with a warning, he'll be back. You know these cocky, arrogant brush jumpers. All they own is a self-sufficient pride. Break that and you put the fear of God in them."

Streak rubbed his chin, thoughtfully taking Channing in from head to foot. Channing knew how he looked: a seedy, ragged, and bearded man of less than average height, and light for that. No more than the tramp Santee had named him . . . yet Streak hesitated. "I'm not so sure . . ."

20

Dyker snorted gently as he stepped back inside the house. Whitey returned with a coiled lasso and kept up his nervous, eager sniggering. Dyker reappeared hefting a long blacksnake; he cracked it once with a pistol-shot report. "Tie his wrists to the railing. Facing it. Ward, give Whitey a hand."

Streak held the gun against Channing's back while Costello and the thin youth jerked Channing's arms above his head and lashed them to the porch rail. "Not like you expected, eh?" Costello hissed close to his ear.

Channing said nothing, did not wince at the bite of ropes or the splintered edge of sun-warm wood digging into his wrists, first thinking, *Steady. You've been whipped before,* and thinking automatically then of his father and the savage birchings of his boyhood. Yet the very memory knotted his guts and made his knees go watery and numb. *Don't let them see it.*

"Let me, Mr. Dyker," Whitey said. The crazed giggle again.

"I think not," Dyker said musingly. "The pleasure will be Streak's . . ."

"No," Streak said flatly. "No pleasure."

"You're like my friend the horseherd, Streak. Proud. Too proud." Dyker spat his words with a flat impact. "There's only one cock of the walk on Anchor Ranch. Me. Remember it." He coiled the rope with a flip of his fist and tossed it. Streak automatically dipped it out of the air and turned it in his hands, scowling.

"Do it," Santee Dyker said coldly. "Fifteen strokes. Lay them on hard."

Channing felt Streak move behind him and grab a fistful of his collar. A savage yank ripped the shirt to his waist and the sun glanced hot against his back. He heard Streak haul a deep breath as he took a few steps back. The blacksnake whistled back and forward, the tip lacing hotly across his shoulders.

"Come now," Dyker said dryly. "We won't count that."

Streak cursed softly and struck again. The lash curled like a burning switch around Channing's side and chest. Once, twice, and three more times. Channing closed his eyes and set his teeth. Streak paused. Dyker's remorseless voice: "That's five. Arm tired?"

Channing stood erect and held the count to nine, then his legs sagged and his senses swam in a painful blur. The blows fell numbly, yet he felt the hurt with each beat of his heart. *Don't. Don't, Pa. I won't touch a gun again, I swear . . .*

Water dashed wet and cold against his face. He tried to get his legs under him and failed. A hand fastened in his hair, yanking his head back.

"Reckon he won't be able to walk . . ."

"Set him on his horse."

"He won't stay there."

"Tie him on."

Somebody cut the ropes and he pitched limply down. Hands dragged him up. Images swam blurrily in his vision. He was straddling leather then with his face bowed in a horse's rank, sweaty mane. Again the taut bite of ropes against his wrists.

"Let him go!"

Something cracked against the horse's hip. Channing felt his head snap back, his body arch agonizingly with the animal's leap. Hoofs churned and his body tossed limply with the motion, his chin bouncing against his chest. It jerked him to half-awareness; he fought to hold that vague sentience, though with it the numbness receded and brought throbbing pain. His vision cleared.

The claybank's pace slackened out. He strained against the ropes binding his wrists to the horn till his fingers closed over the reins. Inching slack into his fists, he gradually guided the animal to a halt. Its flanks heaved; froth slobbered from its mouth. He had pushed the animal hard these last weeks, and against his own misery he dredged up pity. His mangled wrists were bleeding, the sun boiled against his back. He steeled himself against a swimming dizziness, threw all his strength into pulling his hands free. Slowly he slipped one hand free of the taut loops, feeling flesh tear; then he was loose.

Flexing circulation back to his fingers, he looked around. The ranch was out of sight. He matched up a swell of foothills to the north with the terrain he'd mentally mapped earlier, as was his habit in unfamiliar country. To the south would be the wagon road that connected Anchor and the town of Sentinel; he pulled the claybank's head in that direction.

Shortly he struck the shallow bed of a clear stream fed by melted snow from the northern peaks. He dismounted and threw reins to kneel by the cool flow gushing over mossy stones. He cupped his hands and drank. The water was icy, hurting his teeth, shocking him to full sensibility. The stubborn, insensate pride that was in him asserted itself; he was reluctant to head for town and a physician's care. No man whipped like a dog wanted his shame exposed to others. Against that he measured the danger of blood poisoning and infection in the burning wounds that laced his back. Gingerly he shrugged out of his torn shirt. He slowly extended his body full length over the stream as he lowered himself on his hands. The impact of the icy water foaming up around his trunk took his breath away. First it blazed wetly against his lacerated back and then a welcome numbness gently encroached. Running water would cleanse the cuts.

Detachedly, almost drowsily, he considered his next move. He did ask himself whether his ends were changed; they were not. Get Costello, that simple. The whipping had only hardened his resolve. To the indictment of Lacey's death he could add a pure joy of revenge with no conscience-qualm, no squeamishness about method.

He rose, absently toweled his dripping body with his shirt as, drag-footed, he ascended the bank to his horse. He untied and unwrapped the blanket roll, exposing the oiled gunbelt. He strapped it on, feeling its weight on his hip like an old friend. His smile was not pleasant, a mere tightening of set lips over his teeth. He dug a worn ducking jacket which had been Lacey's from his saddlebag. Oversized on him, its loose folds would not irritate his back. He buttoned it to the neck, discarding his ruined shirt.

In fifteen minutes he reached the wagon road and followed it to Sentinel, riding slowly in his dizzy exhaustion. He met nobody on the road. The ashen pallor of dusk had closed over the town when he reached the slapdash clutter of run-down railworkers' shanties on the east out-skirts. He crossed the tracks, rode past the wind-stench of empty stockpens and turned onto the main street. He left his horse at the livery stable with orders for its feed and care, afterward heading for the hotel two blocks down the street, carrying his saddlebags. The leaden exhaustion that pulled at his legs was beginning to hamper all of his movements. His head pounded feverishly. He crossed the hotel lobby and braced himself against the desk as, tight-voiced, he asked for a room and signed the register the curious but discreetly unquestioning young clerk shoved at him.

Up in the narrow and musty cubbyhole of a room he did not light the lamp. He kicked the door shut behind him and paused only long enough to shed the heavy jacket before he lurched to the bed and collapsed across the sagging mattress. Dead, dreamless sleep claimed him almost at once.

CHAPTER
THREE

A finger of sunlight hazed through the fly-blown window and across the faded blanket. It touched Channing's face and he opened his eyes. He winced from belly-down to a sitting position, then eased to his feet. His whole body ached, but inspecting his back in the cracked mirror above the washstand he saw that the broken flesh open to the air had already begun clean healing. Mostly the blacksnake had left discolored stripes, not nearly as bad as he'd expected.

Despite his cramps he felt fit enough. He poured water into the basin, carefully shaved and afterward stripped down and sponged himself clean. He changed to his one pair of clean levis and a shirt, then stepped into the hall, locked his room, and went down to the lobby.

The day clerk, a different and older man, glanced up idly. "Mornin'."

"Mornin'. Can I buy a bait?"

"Our dining room's open nine till midnight, back off the lobby there."

Channing went through the double doors into a long room with a heavy oak table running three-quarters of its length. Each place was set but it was an hour before noon and only one old man was eating. He. looked hunched and runty, alone at the big table. Channing paused in the doorway, watching with faint amusement. The old fellow was eating as though it were the last civilized meal he expected to enjoy, wolfing it down with scalding mouthfuls from his coffee cup. He looked rawhide-lean, rawhide-tough, in a greasy elkhide shirt and leggings. His freshly clipped hair lay close against his lean skull, but a snowy beard still furred his gauntly hollowed cheeks.

He growled surlily without looking up, "Your pap teach you better manners'n to stare?"

"He tried," Channing said dryly, "real hard."

He skirted the table and sat down opposite the oldster. A fat cook in a soiled apron waddled from the kitchen. "Yours?" Before Channing could reply the old man said in the same half-snarled, uncompromising way, "Grub's all spoilt. Try the ham and eggs though."

Channing nodded to the cook, who gave the old man an unnoticed glare and went back to the kitchen. "Name's Channing."

"Brock." The old man snapped his teeth on the name as if he wanted no more talk. Channing guessed him to be a burned-out, broken-down mountaineer down for supplies, one good meal, one good drunk, and his annual shearing — half-dotty with solitude and distrusting every-one. Yet he caught a brief up-flicker of the bright, still-young eyes, saw their shrewd assessment of him before they lowered. He was odd enough, but sane and no fool, Channing knew then. Brock dropped his knife and fork with a clatter on his wiped-up plate, sleeved his mouth and stood up. He tramped from the dining room with a noiseless moccasined tread, not looking back.

"Where's Brock?" It was a young voice, a brash voice carrying clearly from the lobby.

"Here he comes now," was the desk clerk's reply. "Brock, here's Max and Karl wantin' a word with you."

"I know their word, and this child's got no time."

"You got time for this, dad," said the brash voice.

Channing stood and walked to the double doors, halting there. Two men who were evidently brothers blocked the mountaineer's way in the center of the lobby. One was young and stocky with close-cropped pale hair, and Channing knew it was he who'd spoken. The other was an older man of mournful mien, also light-haired and blue-eyed.

"No beating the bush, dad," said the young one. "John Straker wants to see you — out at Mexican Bit. We was up to your shack yesterday. Nobody there, but found your mule's tracks trailin' for town."

"You rid a piece for nothin'," Brock grunted, and started to walk around the pair.

The youth clapped a meaty hand solidly on the skinny shoulder. "Don't reckon. Karl, get on his other side." The sad-faced one reached out a long arm and caught Brock's.

"Damn your liver and lights! Straker wants to talk, he kin ride up the high country same's the trash he hires," Brock bristled.

"No trouble, dad. Make it easy, all round."

"Let him go."

Channing sidled easily through the doors as he spoke, came across the puncheon floor. He stopped two paces away, weight balanced on the balls of his feet. Half-poised because he could read the way of this in Max's arrogant, wild grin. He sized them up as a salty pair but not hardcases.

Max dropped Brock's arm, rubbed his hands together. "Watch the crowbait, Karl. I ain't had breakfast." He rushed, bulling in with his head down. Channing stepped aside and chopped his right fist in a short, savage arc that ended behind Max's ear. He crashed to the floor, lunged to his feet at once and spun after Channing, who hit him off-balance even as he wheeled. Max back-pedaled, thick legs churning for footing. Channing followed up, belted him under the chest, and when Max straightened, teetering precariously on his heels, Channing brought his open hand up from his waist. Its calloused heel clouting Max's jaw rocked him back in an arching fall. He looked up glassily, wagging his head.

Channing half-turned, leveling his lidded stare on Karl "You had breakfast?"

"Oh, sure," Karl said mournfully. He walked almost gingerly to Max and helped him to his feet. Max kept his baffled gaze on Channing. He rubbed his jaw, saying with no truculence, "You Anchor? Spur, maybe?"

Channing shook his head in flat negation. "Better get out. Fast."

When the lobby doors had closed behind them the mountaineer's agate-bright gaze swung on Channing.

There was no relenting in his snarl. "Who you softenin' me for?"

"You been sizing me," Channing said coldly. "Seen me before?"

Brock dropped his prickly stare to the gunbelt. "Wagh, it fits you're hired talent."

"Old man, I don't know about your feuds here. Nor give a damn. Believe that or don't."

Brock fingered his beard. "I believe it," he said with surprising mildness. "Thought I cut your drift, hoss. Even liked it. But you can't never be sure about a man."

With this calm jot of cynicism he turned and padded silently out through the street door. The desk clerk whistled softly. "That's something, mister. Old Brock don't fancy nobody . . . but he likes you."

"Who is he?"

"Old trapper — mountain man, last of his kind. First white man in these parts . . . forty year and more ago. Stiff-necked as hell."

"I saw that," Channing said impatiently. "He's got something a lot of folks want."

The desk clerk's sallow face lowered nervously; he aimlessly fingered the open register. "Look . . . don't know you. You say you're disavowed with Spur or Anchor, fine, but you might take sides. Me, I stay out, clean out."

Channing hesitated and shrugged. It was no mix of his either, no point pushing his curiosity with nothing at stake. He went back to the dining room and sat down to a platter of ham and eggs. He wolfed it ravenously, washed it down with three cups of coffee that was black and caustic. Feeling physically better with himself and the world, he went back to the lobby and selected a leather chair with the horsehair padding leaking out. He pulled it around facing the front window and slacked down, wincing his back to a comfortable position. He stared idly at the saloon opposite the hotel with the sign across its blank, windowless upper story nearly weathered away: JUDD'S — LIQUOR AND TUDD'S.

He toyed with a miscellany of notions on making Ward Costello pay the piper . . . and Anchor Ranch. His brows knitted in a frown; there were cross-currents in this basin which might prove rewarding to investigate. He at once discarded the idea; he'd lone-wolfed it too long; his ways were direct, not intriguing.

A stutter of hoofbeats pulled his attention to the window again . . . two riders heading in, leading a riderless horse. He glanced, over at the clerk, who circled the desk and came to the window, peering out. "Saturdays some of the boys from the three big outfits come in to see the elephant." He chuckled enviously. "Happen two of 'em crowd in at once, they'll be a town-treein' before night-fall."

Channing stood and walked to the window, hands rammed in his hip pockets. "That's a big fella." He jerked a nod at the tall, bull-shouldered man just pushing through the swing doors of the saloon opposite. Behind him clumped a short, thickset man with an empty right sleeve neatly rolled and pinned above his shoulder stump.

"That's Bob Thoroughgood — Spur foreman. Other's his *segundo*, Shiloh Dawes."

The approach of four more riders from the opposite end of the street drew Channing's gaze. He recognized the pair in the lead — Streak and the kid called Whitey . . .

"That's —" the clerk began with relish before Channing's flat, "I know them," bit off his speech short.

Channing watched stiffly as they dismounted. He had not been prepared for the cold, feral rage that flooded him at seeing Streak. The man who'd whipped him had been acting under orders, had even been reluctant. It might be the arrogant way Streak sat his saddle or the quiet cocksureness of his lean face — but Channing knew abruptly what he was going to do.

The four riders were scanning the hip-brands on the two horses tied at the rail as Channing stepped from the hotel. He crossed the street as the riders filed into the saloon; he went in on the heels of the last man.

The one-armed *segundo* glanced around, his voice quiet and dry: "Roll out the red carpet, Doc. Streak and the boys are in."

"Man drinks where he chooses, free country," the bartender said tersely. He was a stout man with a head bald as a cue-ball, wearing thick spectacles incongruous with his tough, doughy face.

"So's the air in it," Whitey giggled. "Clean air, up to now . . ."

32

"Free inside limits," Doc said ponderously. He grunted over, and came up with a sawed-off Greener which he laid lightly across the bar. "Leave the hatchet in the street or clear the house. The damn lot of you."

"Slack off, Whitey," Streak said irritably. "The usual, Doc."

"The same." Channing elbowed in, crowding the Anchor foreman aside.

"Why, that's —" Whitey began, but Streak made a chopping motion with his hand that cut the kid off. Streak turned slowly, resting an elbow on the bar as he faced Channing, with less than a foot between them.

"You should've been gone, brush jumper, way gone," he said softly, wickedly.

"Maybe you want to argue that?"

Faint puzzlement shaded Streak's bleached eyes; they flicked down at the holstered Colt on Channing's hip. "Why —" he hesitated, puzzled but unafraid — "I'm not just sure . . ."

Channing glanced down at the glasses which Doc was sloshing full. "Maybe this'll make up your mind." He moved one hand to lift a glass in an unbroken movement, throwing the contents in Streak's face. Streak choked, cursed wildly as he backed against the man behind him. Very slowly he raised his arm to wipe the liquor away. He blinked his eyes clear; Channing was now standing well out from the bar facing them all. The violence in Streak's face thinned to wariness. He straightened from his half-crouch, letting his breath out.

"I was right about you," he said huskily.

"It was a mistake."

"A mistake." Streak added wickedly, "I don't back-water. Don't think that!"

Channing nodded unconcernedly as though it meant nothing. "I'm handing my gun to the apron. You do the same."

"That's good, brush jumper." Streak breathed the words, his grin chalk-white. He unbuckled his shell belt and laid it on the bar, not once taking his eyes off Channing. Only when Streak had moved from the bar did Channing shuck his own belt and gun. He tossed it to the bartender and moved after Streak.

"Take it outside, you roosters," Doc growled, but it was too late. Still coming forward, Channing aimed a straight left from the shoulder; it glanced off Streak's cheekbone. The Anchor foreman grunted and bored in. Channing ducked beneath his full-arm swing. He grabbed Streak around the waist, lifted, threw his hip behind the man's right buttock and swung him off his feet. He brought his own weight atop Streak as they crashed to the floor. A wrestling throw learned from a half-Apache wrangler of his, its unexpectedness, had caught Streak off guard.

Channing could feel the straining power in Streak's lean, wiry body as he fought to throw off the mustanger's pinning weight, and knew then that he had a wildcat on his hands. Streak wasn't much bigger than he but the foreman's prideful, near-cocky manner showed him to be used to an easy dominance over tough ones — a right a frontiersman won only by fists or guns, and Streak was no gunhand.

34

Channing had the hold he wanted now — right hand clamping Streak's left arm, forcing it slowly behind his back while his weight, smothering Streak's side and moving onto his back, was forcing the foreman belly-down where he would be helplessly pinned. Streak's body was set in straining resistance, lank hair falling over his eyes. Then, with the sudden canniness of a tempered brawler who could improvise against unknown tactics, he relaxed, throwing his body in the direction Channing was pushing. The unexpected move carried Channing with it, hurling him off-balance. With a quick twist Streak broke the hold and kept turning his body, rolling Channing off him.

Both men were on their feet at once. Channing knew respectful caution now of Streak's lithe speed and saw a like emotion mirrored in Streak's face. They circled slowly with hands spread and bodies crouch-bent. Streak aimed a lightning kick, his boot grazed Channing's hip as the mustanger moved aside; his hands blurred to grab Streak's foot and twist. Streak spun with the twist to keep balance; he crashed against a flimsy deal table and it fell on its side, carrying two chairs with it. But Streak kept his feet. He took two steps and dived, catching Channing around the waist. The impact carried both backward, the swing doors parting to dump the locked men across the sidewalk. Pain tore across Channing's back.

Streak's head was buried in Channing's shirt-front; savagely he knuckled the mustanger's spine. Channing arched upward, grunting with the pain. He tried to pry Streak away and failed. He grabbed a handful of

Streak's long hair and yanked his head back; with the heel of his free hand he pumped three long slogging blows into Streak's jaw. Streak let go and Channing heaved viciously and unseated him.

They scrambled to their feet Channing started to place his weight, but Streak's wild swing caught him flush on the chin. The world exploded in Channing's eyes, and he was falling . . . struck the dirt of the gutter on his back. Streak's boot sank into his side and he rolled blindly from the knifing pain. He heard horses snort and prance and choking dust seared his nostrils; he'd rolled between the tied animals.

He sat up as his head cleared, hearing Streak's savage curse. Now Streak was ducking under the tie rail to reach him. It was brief respite, enough for Channing to rally one deep breath. He gathered his feet under him, squatting; then his body uncoiled, as Streak straightened up. He brought the blow from the ground and it glanced off Streak's cheekbone and staggered him against the tie rail. They stood in the narrow space between the horses' sweating flanks, slugging it out toe to toe, the crude science of common experience forgotten in savage abandon.

Channing was jarred back to sanity by the sharp, salty flow behind his broken lips. He gave back a step and then as Streak moved after him, timed a low punch under Streak's guard and deep into his rigid belly. It was enough to half-double the Anchor man, and Channing brought his other fist to Streak's head in fast combination. Streak tried to counter, but Channing pressed him back to the tie rail, feeling Streak's blows lose force, the dazed shuffle to his movements.

Channing felt the pull of exhaustion weighting his own punches, yet he struck again. Streak's head rocked but he was involuntarily braced upright by the crosspole. Channing let his whole weight carry behind the last blow and his fist and then his shoulder caught Streak's upper body with a bruising force that flopped the foreman over the pole. He went asprawl on his face with legs falling across the sidewalk.

Held wordless during the brutal fracas, the men crowded on the sidewalk broke into talk. It was hushed and murmurous. This had been no whoop-up brawl to release steam; lasting no more than five minutes, it had unleashed a singleminded viciousness that each man felt.

Channing leaned his weight on the tie rail, drawing in great lungfuls of air. A hand fell on his arm. He looked at Shiloh Dawes. "Son," the one-armed man said gravely and dryly, "damned if I know what you were trying to prove. Drive your stakes deep and hard, though. Give you a hand inside? Like to talk . . ."

CHAPTER
FOUR

Channing poured a second whiskey while the first was still exploding tendrils of heat through his aching body. He downed it at a swallow and nodded his thanks at Shiloh Dawes. The Spur *segundo* was seated across from him, a bottle between them, at a rear table. The Anchor men had loaded their beaten foreman on his horse and left Bob Thoroughgood leaned on the bar, his back to the table.

"Two slugs ought to buy your ears a spell," Shiloh suggested mildly.

Channing eyed him speculatively, seeing a squat keg of a man with white steerhorn mustaches spanning his heavy mastiff jaws. His rough face was tempered with the wisdom of an aging and observant man. "I'm listening."

Shiloh twisted in his chair and motioned with his one arm at Thoroughgood. "Bob, come over here."

The foreman looked irritated, but he started across the room. A large dog lying across his path raised its head and growled. It was a gaunt, powerful beast whose dirty yellow fur blended so neutrally with the sawdust floor that Channing hadn't noticed it Thoroughgood swore at it but gave it a wide berth as he came to the table and sat down. The dog settled its head and kept up a rumbling snarl.

"Ugly sonuvabitch," Shiloh commented. "He came around one night and Doc Willis, the bartender there, fed him and he stayed on. Dassn't nobody get close to him, even Doc."

Thoroughgood cuffed his hat to the back of his head with a hamlike fist. Despite his thick trunk, his belly was lean as a boy's, his hips whittled horseman-spare. His large Roman head with thick, gray-threaded black hair was sharp-featured as a hawk's. There was an odd sensitivity in his reserve, like a man who'd been deeply hurt; this alone spared him a manner of bitter indifference. He said impatiently, "What is it?"

"Like you to meet Ed Channing."

The two exchanged neutral stares. Neither offered to shake hands. Thoroughgood said, his hard face not changing, "What the hell bug's got you now?"

"Need men, good men, don't we?" Shiloh demanded.

"Damn it," Thoroughgood said almost angrily, "you don't want to hire a hand, you want to hire a gun. No; let them make the first move. Only a damn fool *asks* for trouble. No offence," he added, addressing Channing for the first time, "but you laid Streak Duryea in the dust. No one's done that, and he's not a man to forget."

"Didn't guess he was," Channing murmured.

Thoroughgood snorted softly. "And you don't care a damn, that it?"

"That's it" Channing bridled faintly at this man's surly truculence which wasn't even aware of itself.

Thoroughgood stared at him now with reluctant interest. "What's your business?"

"My own."

"Easy, Bob, easy," Shiloh said placatingly, and to Channing: "Just interested in your references. Common practice, you ask a man to work for you."

Thoroughgood frowned but said nothing. Channing toyed with his glass, scowled into it, and then shrugged. "Mostly lately I trapped horses."

"Young man's game, that," Shiloh observed placidly. "Get past twenty-five, your bones brittle up, crack like kindling wood. Couple years you'll be too old to work the rough string."

"Yeah."

"No future there. Man ought to look to his future."

"Spit the meal out of your mouth," Channing said rudely. "No future in what you want me for either. A gun. That's all right Mine'll cost you triple cowhand's wages."

Thoroughgood looked near-apoplectic. Before he could speak, Shiloh said quickly, "Bob, knock his wages off mine for the next year. I want this fella."

"And trouble," Thoroughgood spat.

"Man, don't be a damn mule! Now the first lease is up, trouble will come faster'n we can handle. Fight fire with fire."

Thoroughgood released his breath explosively, shook his head in resignation. To the mustanger: "What's your grudge against Duryea?"

"Fifteen stripes he laid on my back with a blacksnake."

"How in hell he do that, stand still for him?"

"Not hardly," Channing said coldly. "Rest is my business, let it ride."

Thoroughgood stood, and leaned forward with his palms on the table. "All right. I ramrodded Spur a dozen years, kept it clean of guntipping tramps; never thought to see the day I'd take one on, but that's the way of it. Keep that smart tongue in your head and keep your nose clean while you're eating Spur grub." He pivoted on his heel and walked back to the bar.

"He wasn't always this way," Shiloh said low-voiced. "Only after his wife —"

"Not interested. Just want to hear what I'm buying into."

Shiloh summed it up quickly and tersely. Bordering the Soledad basin's north and west ramparts was a long, many-acred strip of the finest grazing land in the Sangre de Cristo foothills. It belonged to an old recluse named Elwood Brock. When the other mountain men of the early days had trapped out this basin, they'd moved on. Only Brock, then a young man, had stayed on, hunting and gold-grubbing, having no contact with other men except for roving bands of Indians who thought him possessed by the holy and left him unmolested. He was an odd one, that was sure, for when government surveyors came through to map this basin thirty years ago, Brock had arranged with them on an apparent whim to buy the whole strip of rich-grassed foothill range that spanned the northwest basin. It had taken all his long-saved fur money and painstakingly panned gold.

The first white settler in the basin had been Custis Thursday, late owner of Spur Ranch. He had developed a thriving outfit south of Brock's strip, but had never succeeded in dickering or threatening the old man into selling him the coveted graze. Later when John Straker had built up his Mexican Bit, a fierce two-way pressure had been laid against the old man. Brock had finally compromised, leasing the land out for a ten-year period to the highest bidder, Custis Thursday. Straker had reluctantly pulled in his horns; Thursday had moved his cattle onto the Strip; and, at first, he had prospered.

Santee Dyker was a shrewd, ambitious johnny-come-lately. Unlike his tough predecessors who'd pulled themselves up by their bootstraps, he'd come to the basin two years ago with money enough to start his cattle-land venture in the biggest way; now he threatened to be a far deadlier rival than Straker.

For the ten years were up, the lease had expired, and the three ranches were gathering their forces for a reawakening of the old feud. In the last few years Thursday had put too many irons in the fire, had found out too late that he knew nothing but cattle. A number of bad investments, perpetrated on the aging cattleman by slick-tongued frauds, had crashed. Spur Ranch was in a bad financial way — and a month ago Thursday, returning at night from town to his ranch, had been shot from ambush by an unknown rifleman. The killer had not been found, and Spur could not raise the five thousand dollars old Brock had demanded for the original lease, though Bob Thoroughgood had sweated to salvage every penny from the old man's abortive investments.

In spite of himself Channing was interested; it explained the two riders' rough treatment of Brock in the hotel lobby — an attempt to coerce the old man into leasing to Mexican Bit. But Brock's troubles were no sweat of his, though he'd taken an odd liking to the old hammerhead. His job was to get Costello, who could stay on Anchor till doomsday if he chose, protected by Anchor guns. Meanwhile, after defeating Streak, Channing knew he'd be a target for all those guns. He could not afford to lonewolf it in the basin any longer; he needed protection of his own, and Spur Ranch would be a refuge while he made his plans.

Voicing part of his thought aloud broke the silence following on Shiloh's explanation: "Those Anchor boys . . . all looked hardcase."

Shiloh swallowed his whiskey and drew his sleeve across his silky steerhorns. "Yeah. Santee started importin' 'em a month ago, getting rid of his old crew for gunnies like Whitey DeVore, Elam Ford, Arnt Chance. All mean-bad. He's buildin' up to take the Strip, even if Brock decides to lease to us or Straker. Puts Brock on a mean spot, but the stubborn old bastard won't leave his mountain shack, though alone up there he's in plenty danger. Santee wants a legal signature on that lease, not carin' how he gets it."

"The law?"

"Hell, son, you know New Mexico Territory. Counties sprawling hundreds of square miles over hell-rough terrain. Sheriff's office is fifty miles away in

Cholla, county seat, cut off from this basin by an arm of the Sangre peaks. Even the railroad don't connect us — ours is just a spur line run up through the river pass by the big cowmen here. No deputy here, we never asked for none. No town marshal. Us big ranches always settled our differences amiable, kept the smaller ones in line. Bunch of us — cattlemen, townsmen — sit in on kangaroo court when someone goes coyote, lock him up in a long hut down the street for a spell — or hang him. One lawman wouldn't mean much anyways was there real trouble."

"Seems you got it," Channing observed. "Who owns Spur now? Thoroughgood?"

"No . . ." Shiloh glanced over at the foreman whose great frame was slumped loosely against the bar, his face in the back-bar mirror scowl-set with dark thoughts. "Bob was a mite peeved when Lawyer Wainwright read the Old Man's will two weeks ago. Bob's been with Cus Thursday eighteen years, foreman a dozen. They worked fine in harness but they was never close . . . hell, old Cus wasn't close to nobody. Never married, kept to himself in the big house — though he let Bob and his wife live there after Bob married. She died couple years ago."

"The will?" Channing prompted.

"Funny thing," Shiloh mused. "The Old Man left everything to someone we never heard of, a K. Nilssen of St Paul, Minnesota. Lawyer wrote this fella, he's comin' out to take over. Fact we're in town to meet the train . . ." Shiloh dipped a turnip watch from inside his frayed ducking jacket. "Due shortly. Noon. What's that name — Nilssen? German?"

"How you spell it?" Shiloh somehow drew a man out with a terse, friendly manner that melted reserve.

Shiloh grunted as he drew a folded envelope from his shirt pocket. "That's the name in the corner . . . got this letter from him a week ago sayin' he was coming . . ."

Channing scanned the awkward block printing. "Nils-sen. Likely out of Sweden, maybe Norway. Lot of 'em settle that north country."

"That's quick namin'," Shiloh said approvingly. "Never knew none of them."

"Lived with a Scandinavian family up in Montana, few years back." Channing clamped his mouth shut, while knowing the senselessness of his hatred for discussing his past; he couldn't help it.

Abruptly the swing doors parted and a woman stepped inside. Channing glanced at her, as did every man in the room. Each — excepting Thoroughgood — gave her a respectful nod or word of greeting. She smiled and nodded back, her gaze lingering on Thoroughgood. "Hello, Bob."

He grunted without looking up. She shook her head slightly and crossed the room to the back table. Shiloh heaved quickly to his feet, saying awkwardly, "Howdy, Miz LeCroix. Sit down?"

"Hello, Mr. Dawes. No, thank you." Channing also stood as she laid a hatbox and some packages on the table and peeled off her gloves. She was a statuesque woman in a fashionable sky-blue suit that matched her eyes — about thirty, Channing judged. She looked at him as she unpinned a small porkpie hat from her high-coiled hair which caught the murky light in richly dark glints of red to gold. "Hello," she said pleasantly. "You're new."

"Ed Channing, new Spur hand," Shiloh offered sparely.

"Anne LeCroix. She owns Judd's place. Judd's dead."

"For a man who talks so much, Mr. Dawes never wastes words." Her curiously direct gaze held Channing's face. "What happened?"

"Ought to see Streak Duryea," Shiloh chuckled.

"Is that so? I've heard these bar heroes talk about cutting Streak Duryea down a notch, never to his face."

Shiloh grinned crookedly. "Channing don't even like to talk."

"I see he doesn't," Anne LeCroix smiled. "What was the trouble, Mr. Channing?"

"Mine, ma'am. Then Streak's."

"I could exercise a feminine prerogative or two and tease you into telling — why, he's blushing." She laughed then, and gathered up her packages. As she turned, her gaze stopped on Thoroughgood and the amusement was gone, replaced by a deep softening. She said very quietly, "Does he ever stop brooding?"

"Not much," Shiloh said soberly.

"He never was one to laugh much — all the same there was a time . . ."

Shiloh nodded, a long-ingrained sorrow relaxing his craggy face. "Needs someone to look after him."

A brisk humor stiffened the womanly gentleness which Channing guessed this woman rarely revealed. "And that's you, Mr. Dawes."

"Yes, ma'am," Shiloh said dryly. "Leastways I try."

She walked over to Thoroughgood and touched his arm as she spoke. Thoroughgood gave her a sidelong glance, shrugged his shoulders and grunted something. She turned away, gave Shiloh a self-deprecating little smile and shake of her head and then disappeared through a rear doorway.

"Hard man," Channing observed.

"No," Shiloh said sharply, then lowered his voice. "Just that — a man gets deep hurt enough, he can't feel anything afterward . . . I talk too damn' much." He creaked heavily around in his chair, raised his voice. "Bob, train's about due."

Thoroughgood nodded and swung out of the bar, Shiloh and Channing falling in behind. A hot, vagrant wind whipped fine dust against their legs as they tramped the long street to the railway depot. The hoot of a locomotive drifted along the tracks. They stood on the dusty platform as the train wheezed in, slowing with a lengthy crash of couplings.

Channing could feel the tense, quickening curiosity of his companions. This new boss, a Midwesterner fresh to cattle country, could change the accustomed rut of their lives drastically . . . Channing felt detached by his personal thread of purpose and therefore almost indifferent.

The lank conductor stepped from the passenger car and helped a woman down. Rather a girl . . . in a drab black dress and straw hat, clutching a shabby carpetbag to her. She faced the grouped men with a prim and un-worried, almost childlike serenity.

Thoroughgood stirred uneasily, his boots rasping on the cinder bed. "No one else this trip, Charley?"

"Sorry." The conductor's grin was not quite a smirk.

Thoroughgood looked blank. Shiloh Dawes hesitated, then stepped doubtfully forward, touching his hat. "K. Nilssen, ma'am?"

She nodded soberly and moved a brisk step closer to Thoroughgood, dwarfed by him. She wasn't over five feet in height but not slight — compactly sturdy in the shapeless austerity of her dress. She had a freshly scrubbed look even after hours on a train, though sweat beaded her upper lip and damply tendriled silken wisps of corn-yellow hair against her temples. Her voice was gently modulated, richly accented in a way familiar to Channing, calling back memories of Gunnar Nordquist's farmhouse in Montana . . . of an immigrant family poor in goods, rich in love and laughter.

"You are Mister Thoroughgood?"

The foreman nodded once, controlling his face with a kind of iron self-possession.

K. Nilssen smiled brightly, looking from one to the other. Suddenly she was no longer prim or drab. "I think we go now, eh, gentlemen?"

CHAPTER
FIVE

Kristina Nilssen had not expected the overnight windfall that had made her owner of a New Mexico ranch, but youth coupled with a not-easy past life and a quick-witted curiosity had made her easily adaptable. "Kristina, you'll take the main chance when it comes, you don't give yourself excuses for being afraid. That's the good way," Papa used to say. "Eric, don't put such things in the girl's head," Mama would scold. "A man it is thinks such a way, not a woman. She will grow up, marry a good, solid young farmer. It's the best a decent girl can hope for."

She'd always favored Papa, Kristina knew, and she found no shame in the fact. Eric Nilssen had had his private dreams, the ones that made life more than just eating and sleeping and having children. He had worked two years to earn his passage to America, not expecting streets paved with gold, only a good fighting chance for himself and his family in a wide-open new land. He had gotten his chance — only to break himself on a gutted dream.

Sitting on the jolting wagon seat, Kristina knotted her fists in her lap, bit her lip in sudden uncertainty. No; she must not think of the past. They were not dead, not Papa or Mama or the dreams, not while she was alive. She had the life they had given her and the hopes and now the main chance and she would rather die trying than live afraid and doubting. What could a woman alone in a strange land do with these things? There was so much she did not know — and she would learn. Kristina braced her spine a little stiffer on the flat hard seat and breathed deeply the piñon-scented air.

Thoroughgood had rented a buckboard at the livery and tied the extra saddle horse to the tailgate with Channing's mount. Channing rode the high seat at her side. Shiloh Dawes and Thoroughgood rode ahead of the team, passing a few words but not many. Kristina's glance fixed curiously on the bull-shouldered back of the foreman, her brows knitted in puzzlement. A strange, gruff man . . . trying to hide the pain he plainly lived with. Yet she thought she liked him. And the old one-armed man too; there was kindness in him.

She couldn't make up her mind about the young one . . . Channing. The seat was narrow and their shoulders pressed together. He looked slim and hard and capable, his muscles flexing in easy co-ordination as he guided the livery team expertly over the rough wagon road. This one would do everything well, she guessed; cold-blooded men usually did. She glanced covertly at his profile, seeing it finely regular but too sharp-planed and brooding. A man with little use for other men, with few human feelings. But was it so? She noted the gentle restraint of his hands on the reins, his occasional low word to the horses. *A man good to animals cannot be bad*, she thought. She sighed a little, half-closing her eyes. She was tired from the long train ride; her thoughts were becoming confused. The afternoon shadows lengthened across the rugged plateau they were traversing, making the shadows of men and horses grotesque moving specters . . .

"We're here, Miss."

"Oh!" Kristina had been half-dozing, and now she felt Channing's shoulder stir against her slumped weight. Flustered, she sat up, reaching under the seat for her carpetbag. But her hand stopped as her eyes took in the rambling slope. Piñon and juniper darkly stippled the brighter greens of aspen and oak, fading back to grassy meadows and higher wooded benches, hazing away to the serrated purple of snow-tipped peaks. She forced her wondering gaze back to the immediate slope, and downward to the wide clearing with its open-sided hayshed, corrals, blacksmith shop, and ten yards down the yard incline the combination bunkhouse and cookshack. She identified all of these at once and then her eyes moved to the house in majestic isolation upslope against a somber backdrop of evergreens. The main structure was an oblong block of mortared fieldstone with two matching wings of heavy timber, built solidly back against the slope behind. She could guess how here beneath the peaks it would be cool in summer, cozy in winter . . . a dwelling that fit the country like a glove over a hand.

"Oh," Kristina Nilssen said once more, now whispering it.

Thoroughgood rapid-fired an order at Channing to see to the wagon and horses, then he took her bag from unresisting fingers and led the way to the house, Shiloh Dawes following. She stepped almost gingerly across the veranda and stopped on the threshold as Thoroughgood held open the door. She couldn't hold back a little exclamation of delight.

The leather furniture was well-worn, but choice and substantial. The walls were hung with game trophies and bright Indian blankets and the oak rafters overhead were smoke-seasoned to a rich brown-black. She moved quickly around the room, paused by the fireplace to draw a finger across the dust on the mantle of the huge yellow-stone fireplace and frown a little. Then her gaze touched with surprise the window curtains, fine cloth but grime-gray and unwashed in months — or years.

She glanced swiftly at Thoroughgood, seeing the bare patience in his stony face. Pride hardened her thoughts. She was the owner now; she would ask the first questions. "When was a woman here, mister? Long ago, eh?"

"How the devil did you —" He checked himself, added tersely, "My wife. Died two years ago."

"Oh." She nodded very slowly, understanding now. Poor man. She smiled at them. "The kitchen —"

"Doorway to your left," Thoroughgood said. "Look — miss —"

"You yust wait. I will make some coffee. Then we talk." He frowned and she said with an edge to it, "I am tired if you are not. *We will not talk until after I have made coffee.*"

Thoroughgood opened his mouth and clamped it shut. Shiloh Dawes glanced at the big man, then turned his face away, but failed to hide his grin from Kristina.

She opened the door and entered the dining room, delightedly taking in the fine oak highboy and the broad, round-topped table. Then her foot struck an empty liquor bottle and it rolled across a floor littered with pieces of harness and heel-ground cigar butts. She made a small dismayed sound, seeing the burns on the table edge where men had carelessly left lighted cigars. She bent to scrub at them with her sleeve, then stopped, gripping the table with her hands. Quite suddenly Kristina felt like crying. She had come a long way, she was very tired . . . and these stupid men! As quickly, she fought the feeling down. Thoroughgood had come to the open door; he gave a surly nod at the table.

"Old Cus and me ate here nights, went over the ranch books afterward. Guess the place is a little dirty." There wasn't a lot of apology in his tone. "I been livin' on here. Better move my stuff to the bunkhouse . . ."

"Yah, you better," she cut him off coldly and marched to the kitchen, her back very straight.

Ten minutes later she carried the coffeepot to a low table fronting the leather divan where Thoroughgood and Dawes were sitting. The one-armed man looked at poor ease, but Thoroughgood had stretched out his legs and leaned back grim-faced, plainly damned if he was going to let a dumb immigrant girl get under his skin. Kristina considered this grimly as she carefully set the steaming coffeepot on a folded newspaper. She was about to begin a sharp-tongued comment when the front door opened. Channing stood there, removing his hat.

"Horses are put up, pulled the wagon out of the way. Anything else?"

"Get your stuff to the bunkhouse, pick out an empty bunk," Throughgood said. "Crew's out fencing, be in shortly for supper. Acquaint yourself with the place till then." It was a dismissal, and Channing turned to leave.

"Wait," Kristina said sharply. "Have some coffee first, mister. Here . . . sit down."

All three men stared at her as though she had calmly announced the final Judgment. She shrewdly guessed at the invisible line between owner's quarters and bunk-house and didn't turn a hair. Let them squirm . . . Men! She casually filled four cups and handed one to Channing as he eased onto the edge of a straight-backed chair.

"That looks very uncomfortable," she said sweetly. "Now the divan by Mr. Thoroughgood —"

"No ma'am, no, thank you, this is fine."

In addition to spiting Thoroughgood she'd wanted to break Channing's moody reserve, and now she felt a trifle ashamed of her success. She sank against the sagging cushions of the divan. Sipped the coffee judiciously, nodded and said briskly: "None of you are drinking."

Shiloh gulped the scalding brew. "Oh, it's mighty fine."

54

"My mother taught me," she said proudly, "though I did no cooking for two years, as a chambermaid in a hotel."

There was an awkward silence, tentatively broken by Shiloh. "That would be St. Paul, ma'am? Take it you met Mr. Thursday there? He was in St. Paul arranging some investments, last year. Figured you might've met him then . . ."

"Yah, he stayed at the hotel," she said matter-of-factly. "He became sick, very sick. All I could I did for him; poor old man. So lonely and trying to cover it with tough words."

Thoroughgood gave a short, explosive "Ha!" She straightened and glared at him. "I am not surprised now, seeing the company he kept, eh? Do not tell me he was a poor rich old man, mister; I knew it, the same I would do for a dog, even you."

Shiloh coughed hastily. "Just a surprise, you inheriting all this, ma'am. Mr. Thursday never mentioning you and all. Course we knew he had no living relatives . . ."

"He had a heart, that you did not know. Or care," she said tartly. She set her cup down and said firmly, "Now you fill your boots, Mister Thoroughgood, and get out what you want to say."

She frowned at the severe dark material of her skirt and fingered her frayed cuffs, listening to the foreman. He rattled off facts and procedures of ranch life with dry tonelessness, speaking very swiftly to confuse her. She would not give him the satisfaction of telling him to speak slowly, but she gleaned an outline of the situation, methodically sorted it for the strong points, and said carefully: "This grass of which the old man is the lessor — it is very urgent we need it?"

"We're finished without it," Thoroughgood said flatly. "Your late benefactor made a lot of bad deals, ran Spur into a hole. We're finished anyway, can't raise even a thousand."

"Yah, and it is five thousand is needed," she said musingly, adding: "I have the money."

Thoroughgood spluttered into his cup and set it quickly down. "You got . . . five . . . thousand *dollars?*"

"Got ten thousand," she said serenely. "A month ago, I got a package from Sentinel, New Mexico, containing ten thousand dollars. There was no name of the sender, no note to explain. I yust put it away and say nothing, think maybe it must be a mistake and the owner would claim it."

"Ten thousand dollars," Thoroughgood muttered. "Old buzzard must have had it salted away . . . or got sudden-lucky on one of his fool investments . . ." She started a frowning objection to his choice of words, but he cut her off excitedly. "You got the money *with* you?"

For answer she reached for her carpetbag and went through her few shabby belongings to produce a neatly wrapped brown paper package, handing it to him. "It all is there."

There was a shining, boyish excitement in the foreman's eyes that pleased her; he was actually smiling. "This is it . . ."

"Sure is," Shiloh said phlegmatically, " 'pending how Brock's temper turns."

Kristina put in, "This old mountain man must be strange, more than Mr. Thursday."

Shiloh grinned at her. "Guess it's that living alone."

She laughed, caught up in the half-suppressed excitement of the men, knowing she was a part of it now. She sobered with a troubling thought "Just how did Mr. Thursday die? You say only he was shot . . . ?"

Thoroughgood said casually, but almost too quickly, she thought, "Oh, a drifter he kicked off the ranch got drunk and laid for old Cus. Grudge killing. We hanged the man."

Kristina was about to question further when Channing cleared his throat, saying quietly, "Guess nobody in particular's in Brock's good graces. Maybe I can help."

Thoroughgood eyed him narrowly. "How?"

"Gave him a hand this morning when a pair tried to rough him — Max and Karl by name —"

"The Mannlich boys, Mexican Bit," Shiloh nodded. "Tough lads, but not mean-bad . . . You thinkin' you might trade on that?"

Channing shrugged. "He liked me some. Maybe, though, he'll think we rigged the other to set this up."

"No matter, worth a try," Thoroughgood clipped out. "All right, Channing. You'll ride up to see Brock first thing tomorrow. Shiloh, you make out with the old recluse all right, don't you?"

"Says howdy when we meet, more'n most get from him," Shiloh said dryly.

"Get your sleep. You'll be showing Channing the trail up there."

CHAPTER
SIX

Thoroughgood's intensity of mood hadn't abated by the following morning, but his good humor had. He roused Channing and Shiloh out while the crew snored on in their blankets. In the dim light his hawklike features looked fine-drawn and nervous. He paced impatiently back and forth as they dressed.

"Hellfire, Bob." Shiloh's voice was still thick with sleep. "Ease down . . ."

"*You* step it up," was the irritable rejoinder. "I couldn't much give a damn while it looked hopeless. Now there's a hope, got to strike with hot iron."

Shiloh paused in the act of awkwardly yanking on his left boot. "How far you thinking they'll go?"

"Getting soft in the head? Straker's men tried to grab the old man off in town in broad daylight. Santee's more cautious but when he moves, man as lief poke a five-foot rattler." He stopped pacing and swung to face them. "Cookie's packed a lunch, it's in your saddlebags. Your horses are outside."

Shiloh stomped his boot firmly on, heaved to his feet and picked up his rifle from the foot of his bunk, sighing, "Well, hearty headaches," as he clumped out of the bunk-house, Channing behind.

As they swung into leather, Thoroughgood stepped to Channing's stirrup and handed up a thin leather billfold. "There's a thousand . . . dickering money. Dicker damn well."

Channing tucked the billfold inside his shirt. "Sure you trust me?"

"No," the foreman said bluntly. "I trust Shiloh. Get a move on . . ."

They swung from the ranch yard and, once past the last shed, pointed north toward the blue-toothed arch of the Sangre de Cristos. Glancing back, Channing saw a small figure muffled in an oversized maroon robe on the front veranda of the big house. *Well, she knows, knows what's riding with this and has the sense to be worried.*

But she could not really know — this girl fallen heiress to a great ranch because she had given a loveless and brittle old bachelor his one taste of a woman's unselfish kindness. Thoroughgood had dissembled to her query of how Custis Thursday had met his death, in an attempt to keep her ignorant of the deadly nature of the triangular rivalry; he evidently feared that a woman, once knowing the facts, would not stand the gaff of range war. But she could not be deceived forever. The foreman was trying to preserve Spur Ranch intact for her; though Channing felt strong distaste for the deception, he reminded himself that it was no business of his. Yet he had seen cattle war in the Tonto Basin and in Lincoln County; all the ingredients for pitched warfare were here, and the edged tensions razoring a thin leash. Once one side had cinched an advantage —

Brock's lease — violence would break openly . . . the night-riding, the shots from ambush, the cut fences, burnings and stampedes, and Channing felt the marrow-deep sickness won of experience . . .

The sun topped the east horizon and slanted warm against their right sides. They mounted deeper into the high country. The land became more rugged, the timber of hardier variety. Belts of fir and cedar were interspersed with grassy benches and meadows. This was old Indian and Spanish country, still unviolated by axe or plow, and the morning was beautiful. Squirrels chattered in the dappled foliage and long-tailed mountain jays flashed through shadow and sunlight. On the open stretches grazed isolated bunches of cattle which spooked from their coming. Old Indian and game trails crisscrossed high into the foothills; these they followed, Shiloh picking the way unhesitatingly.

"Two more hours to Brock's cabin," Shiloh threw back over his shoulder as he humped his whey-belly mare over a deadfall.

"He high up?"

"Pretty deep in the foothills, but short of the first peaks. What you think of Miss Nilssen?" Without waiting for a reply, he chuckled, "Damned if she didn't have old Bob buffaloed. She'll make out. If all Swedes is like her, I'd hate to run afoul of the menfolk."

"Most of 'em," Channing said judiciously, "are like friendly mules . . ."

"Son, no such thing as a friendly mule." Shiloh guffawed. "She brought luck, that's sure." He added softly and soberly, "Bob was like a kid, last night. Haven't seen him this way in years."

"Been with him long time?"

"Sojered under, him in the war. Saved my life at Shiloh . . . where I lost this wing." With pride he told how Lieutenant Thoroughgood had left the breastworks to dash through a hail of fire and carry his fallen sergeant to safety. Grapeshot had riddled Dawes' arm. Shiloh was certain that the lieutenant had saved his life not once, but twice: the overworked Confederate medicos were killing more soldiers from hasty amputation than the enemy had killed outright. So Thoroughgood had commandeered a captured Union surgeon and stood by with a cocked pistol while he'd performed a careful removal of Dawes' arm and fashioned a permanent stump. After the war Shiloh had thrown in his lot with Thoroughgood and had rarely left his side since. "That was young Thoroughgood," Shiloh said meditatively. "Was his wife's death dropped the bottom out of his life. The hurt was two years healin' . . . then he needed something he could set his teeth in, a purpose. He's got it. Him and me and Miss Nilssen was up till all hours last night. Bob was full of plans . . . wants to bring a herd of shorthorns from El Paso, throw 'em on the Strip —"

"Shorthorns? Man, they're a short-legged heavy breed. Throw them up in this rough country, they'll break their legs, get hung up in brush . . . and sure not weather the winters. Graze is too thin —"

"The Strip ain't so high, got rocky bluffs skirting it mostly. Natural fence lines and windbreaks against blizzards. And the grass! . . . A cattleman's dream, Channing. And it ain't yet been worked to potential. Aside from them fool investments of his, Custis Thursday was too set in his ways. Bob's got his dreams, willing to gamble." Shiloh jogged a way in thoughtful silence, said, "So's Santee Dyker. An honest-to-God gambler from the Mississippi riverboats. And that could . . ."

It could leave the Strip soaked in blood, Channing thought, and the two men held silence afterward, each with his thoughts . . .

Short of high noon they topped a rise. Beyond dipped a brushy vale and high on a rocky shoulder of its opposite slope was a cabin of green peeled logs. They paused to blow their horses. No sign of life . . . the chimney was smokeless; the sun-drenched stillness seemed to brood.

"Brock's?" Channing laconically broke the talkless two hours.

Shiloh's eyes were narrowed. "Could be out hunting, checking a trapline stream," he muttered, but Channing knew he felt it too as the *segundo* grunted brusquely, "Let's get up there."

They dismounted in the bare, trampled clay of the yard and Channing gave the scarred earth one scanning glance. He said quietly: "Brock got more'n one horse?"

"No horses. One old yellow mule." Shiloh cut his speech off sharply, glancing at Channing. "What —"

Channing was already moving through the doorway where the split-log door hung ajar on deerhide hinges, ducking beneath the low jamb. He stopped in his tracks. The room was meagerly furnished with a wooden bunk, a half-log table, a bench and a stone fireplace. Gear, traps, hides, and a Winchester long rifle hung on the walls, all with an air of tidy economy in ill-keeping with the bed-clothes wadded in a heap on the packed-clay floor by the stripped bunk.

"Grabbed him outen his sleep," Shiloh breathed. "Otherwise they'd never 'a got inside a half mile of the place without the old mountain man cutting them out."

Channing went outside to decipher the trampled ground. His mustanger's eyes found the tracks of four horses and three men who had entered the shack. Inside of a minute he knew every vital statistic except the horses' color and the identities of two of the men. He'd followed Bee Withers for two weeks, and knew that gimpy, toed-in stride at once.

Shiloh returned from an inspection of the brush corral at the back, reporting, "Brock's mule's still in."

"They set him on an extra horse," Channing said slowly. "Bee Withers and two others . . ."

Shiloh stared at him. "Anything else? — and who the hell is Bee Withers?"

"One of the others might be Streak Duryea, from what I saw of his walk — but Withers makes it Anchor sure." Without more comment, Channing walked to his horse and mounted, and Shiloh stood for a flat-footed moment, then cursed and walked grim-faced to his mount. He yanked his rifle from the boot and checked the action.

"Don't pack a hand gun?" Channing regretted his unthinking words even before, Shiloh swung around, bristling. "Handle this kicker better'n any man I've met, understand?"

Channing nodded mutely, putting his horse into motion. He realized that handling a rifle one-handed was something personal and prideful to Shiloh Dawes, yet was surprised that the mild-spoken *segundo* had taken his thoughtless words as a near-insult.

The kidnappers had struck due west over country that grew progressively more rocky and rugged, laced with long shale slopes and crumbling slides. Channing worked from horseback at a slow pace, frequently dismounting to check an uncertain sign. Often he lost it altogether and had to work the backtrail in concentric circles. It was slow and dogged work; sweat darkened his shirt as much with centered effort as with the rising heat of midday. He held patience; Shiloh did not, fuming with each fresh delay and bridling with the over-all pace.

Well past noon, Channing rose from the ground-check and announced, "They swung at right angles here, cutting south, and the sign's plain. So far it's been the throw-off. Now they're heading for home territory. Doesn't add they'd risk taking the old man straight to Anchor."

"Well?" Shiloh grated.

"You know the lay of the land."

Shiloh cuffed his greasy horsethief hat to the back of his head and squinted at the sun. "We're north of Anchor now. Straight south there's an old line shack, off the beaten way and not much used. Reckon they could hold him there."

"That's probably it."

"Then let's crack it. They got a lead of hours on us. Damn, anything could've happened by now!"

Late afternoon had mellowed to lengthy shadows when they topped a brush-covered ridge which fell away sharply to a small, timbered valley. Wordlessly Dawes pointed toward the trees hugging the base of the ridge. Channing made out the gray roof of the line shack, but little else for the dense trees crowding the building and its corral and outsheds. Wind whipped grimy tatters of smoke from the chimney.

"A hot supper," Shiloh observed dryly. "Maybe Brock's last"

"Unless we work this right" Channing opened and closed his fingers, sweaty against his palms. He knelt and scooped up a handful of gravel, mechanically rubbing it between his hands as he studied the sheer ridge walls that almost ringed the valley. At the far side from where they stood, the cliffs were broken down in a long slide which he guessed formed the only trail down to the valley floor. Trees and underbrush grew sparse between the cabin and that end of the valley. "Doorway on the other side of the cabin?"

"Yeah, and a window."

"Come in by the trail, we'll be spotted. No percentage in cutting down on 'em from these heights. Be a stand-off, and we might hit Brock."

"So?"

Channing's gaze narrowed down on the almost straight-away fall sheering off from the liprock at his feet. "I got to get up by the cabin without being seen.

Only chance . . ." As he spoke, he was turning, lifting the coiled lariat from his saddle. He looped the noose over the horn and threw the coils over the cliff. The fifty-foot rope snaked down the facerock, its tip falling about nine feet short of the base. He took a secure grip on the rope, saying, "Steady him. He'll stand for you."

Shiloh moved to the horse's head and watched worriedly as Channing braced his feet on the rim and swung his full weight outward. The claybank fiddle-footed against the taut rope, but quieted to Shiloh's hand and voice. Channing went down the rope hand over hand in a vertical backward walk, knowing his descent would be cut off from the rear shack window by the heavy foliage below. He reached the end of the rope, flexed his knees and dropped to a springy needle carpet. He palmed his gun and moved at a crouch through the trees till the log walls of the shack grew into view. He moved nearer the building and then ran noiselessly the remaining dozen feet. He sank low against the wall beneath the single small dingy square of window, his heart pounding. A smacking sound drifted sharp through the cracked pane.

"Brock," Streak Duryea's nasal voice came drawlingly, "this goes against my grain. Don't make it rougher."

"Hoss," Brock's cracked voice was tonelessly steady, "there's a time us old-timers quartered sonsofbitches like you for lobo-bait."

Then Whitey DeVore's snigger: "Old turnip's still got the bark on. Hell, Streak, he's tougher'n whang leather . . . got to soften it."

"Not your way," Streak said in a brittle voice.

"Shooting a man in the back's all right, though?" Whitey sneered. "Man, she's hot. Shoved her in an hour ago. Now look . . ." There was a grating of iron. Channing yanked off his hat, risked lifting his head to eye-level at the window sill. Brock was tied to a chair, his rock-set face swollen with bruises, nose and mouth bleeding. Streak, hipshot and with thumbs hooked in his belt, narrowly watched Whitey fasten a gloved hand around a poker handle protruding from the broken isinglass window of a black potbellied stove. He drew the poker out, the end glowing cherry red. Bee Withers leaned with folded arms against the wall by the door, watching this with a painful, vapid grin through his broken jaw. Whitey straightened, swung around with the poker.

"Be careful where you wave that damned thing!" Streak said sharply.

Still sniggering, DeVore walked to the dirty dishes on the table and laid the poker gently across a chunk of raw beefsteak. The sharp sizzle brought Brock's head up.

Whitey's face twitched frenziedly. "Oh, that got him, that got him. Come on, Streak, they ain't no sweatin' him. Lemme —"

Channing came erect, swinging his fisted gun at the window pane. It shattered; a shard nicked his hand as he thrust it through. In the rage that rocked his mind he gave no order, hoping they'd break. Streak's hand slashed to pistol butt as he pivoted toward the window.

Channing shot him in the right shoulder, the slug's impact twisting him with a crash against the wall.

Channing swung back to cover the others: Whitey had already flung the poker at the window; Channing ducked as it cleared his head by inches, sailing on into the brush. He lunged up in time to see Whitey break for the open door, veer sharply outside and out of sight.

Channing wheeled, ran along the wall to skirt the corner as DeVore reached the opposite corner, and they faced each other across the cabin's length. Whitey's gun was out and Channing fired on the instant Whitey was slammed back, his legs pedaling. His hat rolled off, lips skinned back from his teeth as he fought for footing. Channing held fire, waiting for him to go down. He saw the tightening of Whitey's finger on the trigger. His shot merged with DeVore's. Whitey went down, his legs kicking sporadically. Then he was still.

The shattering echo of a rifle and Bee Withers' stuck-pig squeal brought Channing around. White powder smoke bloomed high on the ridge wall to his right. Turning, he saw Bee Withers leaning far out the window Channing had quitted, his hands clapped to his face. His gun lay on the ground. He had been about to shoot Channing from the side, and now the mustanger looked back at the rocky crest and saw Shiloh Dawes, a stumpy figure against the skyline, lift his rifle and wave it once.

Channing motioned him to come down, and went around to the doorway. Streak was on his hands and knees, gasping his pain as he tried to scoop his gun into his good hand. Channing stepped into the room and sheathed his weapon as he kicked Streak's beyond his reach.

Streak slumped like a tired child against the wall, breathing hoarsely as he stared up with bright-shot and hating eyes. "Damn Indian," he whispered.

Withers was still hunched over the window sill, groaning; Channing grabbed him by the shoulder and turned him, pulling his hands down. Withers' sallow face was bleeding in half a dozen places from thrown splinters chewed from the outer wall by Shiloh's close-laid slug. Otherwise he wasn't hurt, but was too slow-witted to realize it. Channing shoved him over by Streak, pulled his pocket knife and unfolded the blade. He cut Brock's ropes.

The old man stood a little shakily, but briskly rubbing his skinny wrists as he swung his glare about. "Where's that goddamn poker?"

"Take it easy."

"This child lived with the Blackfeet up north in the early days. Learned a trick or so as'd turn that cub's hair white if it wasn't. Where is the bastard?"

His eyes fixed on Channing's face and something he saw softened his piercing glare. "Wagh. Dead, eh?"

"Him or me."

"Don't look to me like the world's nohow ended, fact it's a sight cleaner without that one. Couldn't tell that from your face, though."

Channing's fingers flexed lightly over the Colt butt; he let his hand drop. *You draw lightning once,* he thought, *and you can't turn back.* He had been fool enough to think he could escape it once, mustanging in

69

the lonely hills, only to find himself embroiled again. Once a man drew trouble in this raw country, it marked him. Like the brand of Cain his father had always been fond of throwing up to him.

In his mind's eye he saw that rawboned, black-suited figure — his father — moving for him with self-righteous anger. He remembered clearly that day long ago when his uncle, returning from a hunting trip, had stopped at their house on one of his rare visits. Leaving his gun leaning against the porch outside because the old man wouldn't permit firearms under his roof. And he, young Eddie Channing, bare brown toes squishing through the hot dust as he sidled up, fascinated by the shiny weapon. Then the forbidden fruit was suddenly hot and hard in his palms and he was drawing a mock bead on a knot-hole in the porch planking. Somehow the flat explosion of the rifle and a slamming recoil sprawling him in the dust . . . his father's hand grabbing the scruff of his neck like iron and dragging him to his feet. *I have warned you about these tools of Satan, boy. Now I shall impress the lesson. They that take the sword shall perish by the sword.*

Scripture had always rolled glibly off the old man's tongue; it had been at once his fortress, his book of common law, and his excuse. Fortified behind the zealot's asceticism, he'd had no tolerance for the ordinary weaknesses of flesh. His son was the only scapegoat within his reach, the target for the punishment he couldn't wreak on the great sin-ridden Gomorrah which was the world as he saw it. Dimly the boy had understood this even then; it had not etched the savage birching less deeply in his memory . . .

"Hoss," old Brock said quietly, the very calmness of the word shocking Channing back to the present. His body felt clammy, trembling with the knowledge that he'd taken another life. His father's words lay on his mind like a cold indictment: *They that take the sword* . . .

The reaction was brief; he walled it off in his mind, again cold and resolved to the business at hand as Shiloh Dawes came huffing through the door. "All right, Brock? Good . . . I worked around on the ridge till I could ketch a sight of the shack where the trees grew low." He grinned unpleasantly at Bee Withers. "Had to take a jiffy bead. Too damned . . . Well, Brock, how d'your notions set?"

The ancient mountaineer stroked his beard thoughtfully. "Looks like you ran out of competitors. This child's tired o' threats from the other two. Cold cash sets easier on a man's sweetbreads than hot iron. That's," he added fiercely, "if ye got the cash."

CHAPTER
SEVEN

Brock and Shiloh alternately cursed him for a damned fool; Channing ignored their acid objections as he treated Streak Duryea's shoulder with bluestone and sweet oil he'd found in a cupboard. Streak was silent through the ministrations, face drawn with tight-held pain and a chilling hatred. Once he snarled, "Do unto others, eh, bucko? Oh, I'll remember. *Bueno*, I'll return the favor — with interest."

Channing tore a strip from a cot blanket and bound up the wound. "That'll hold you till Anchor." He ordered Withers to help Streak outside, then went ahead to tie Whitey's body across his saddle. Flanked by the two old men, he watched them head out.

Shiloh began a surly complaint: "We'd of been within our rights —"

"Sure," Channing said harshly. "And Brock wanted to burn 'em a little. Even Streak didn't want that for him before. I just know to me right is right and wrong is wrong. I wonder what the hell's the matter with me."

Shiloh growled under his breath, but Brock's wise and faded eyes met Channing's without wavering. "No one's sayin' it ain't, hoss," he observed mildly. "Only you toss bones to a pack that's tryin' to pull you down.

Streak, there, now — no mean *hombre* till things don't go his way. Primed to do wuss'n burn *you* now. Anchor's whole pack of curly wolves'll be lookin' to nail your hide after this. Walk soft, they'll dance on your grave. Keep your primin' dry, hoss."

It was well after dark when the trio reached Spur. They corraled their horses and headed up to the house. Thoroughgood and Kristina Nilssen were waiting for them on the porch, limned in the light that flowed from the open doorway. The old mountain man was half-reeling with exhaustion and the punishment he'd absorbed, but he angrily brushed aside proffered hands as he stamped across the porch. ". . . Damned molly-coddlin' fools!"

Kristina followed him inside, her eyes flashing and lips set. "You will please take care of your words under my roof."

Brock turned to face her, his cantankerous expression altering sheepishly. "Wagh. Young gel, eh? Fact is didn't see you, Missy. Figured new lady owner these hosses mentioned was some dried-up ole maid friend of Cus'."

A slow smile dimpled the corners of Kristina's mouth. She was wearing a worn and wash-faded calico dress which faithfully outlined two pointed little breasts and a slim waist before it flared into a full skirt. Her blonde hair was drawn to a smooth bun at the back of her neck and she looked trim and altogether charming. "That is accepted, Mr. Brock. But we had not expected the pleasure of your company . . . ?"

"He decided to come in, deal with you direct" This from Shiloh, who had already warned Brock to say nothing of what had happened.

Thoroughgood cleared his throat "Better get this lease business settled now."

A little frown pinched Kristina's smooth forehead. She said dryly, "Mr. Thoroughgood is minded of nothing but business, eh? First we eat," and firmly closed the discussion by leading the way into the dining room. Thoroughgood released a resigned sigh, but Channing caught a faint smile on his thin lips. Kristina had won these blunt men with a bluntness of her own more charming than any feminine wile.

After supper Kristina cleared away the dishes while the men self-consciously fired up some fine cigars of Custis Thursday's which Kristina had found on a top pantry shelf and which she insisted the men smoke up. She sat by and shrewdly offered no comment in men's talk as Brock opened the deal by naming a price well above the expected five thousand. Thoroughgood made his bid well below and worked up to a compromise at five thousand. At seven cents an acre, Spur would again take possession of the Strip for ten years, making all due efforts to keep it clear of rattleweed, larkspur and the like. In the morning they would see Lawyer Wainwright in Sentinel and have the necessary paper drawn up.

Brock was half-nodding before they concluded. Kristina installed him in Thoroughgood's former room for the night The foreman, Shiloh and Channing took their way toward the bunkhouse. Halfway there, Thoroughgood halted Shiloh with a hand on his arm.

"Let's have the real story. You fooled the girl by saying Brock's face got that way when his horse threw him. Only Brock don't own a horse. Enough moonlight so I could tell he rode in on a strange animal . . . what happened?"

Shiloh told him gravely, finally adding, "Bob, you sure you're wise holding back the ugly parts? To her this is all just sharp business dealin'. The truth'll be a shock."

Thoroughgood rubbed his chin. "Maybe you're right. Best she hears it from us. She's got rawhide in her, that girl, reckon she could take it." There was a touch of pride in his voice. He was silent a moment, then brusquely: "Once we got Brock's mark on that lease will be soon enough. Committed so far, she'll be less likely to back down."

"Could be," Shiloh said quietly. "But can't say my mind rests easy for this deceivin', for her own good or no. I'm just sayin' don't wait too long on tellin' her."

Next morning Brock was fiddle-fit, in his own words; he mounted to the buckboard seat by Kristina with commendable agility, taking up the reins and clucking the horses into motion. Thoroughgood and Shiloh Dawes and Channing paced the rig on horseback. Thoroughgood had offered no explanation as to why he wanted Channing to accompany the party to town and Channing hadn't questioned the order. All that remained was the signing and witnessing of the lease;

Thoroughgood must believe that Santee Dyker would somehow try to block it.

When they reined up by the two-story business building where Lawyer Wainwright had his office, Santee Dyker was waiting, lounging indolently in a chair against the clap-boarded front. A copperbottom bay with an Anchor brand was tied at the rail; Santee appeared to be alone. Channing flicked his gaze up and down the street: there could be men behind those very windows across the way waiting to cut down on the party. No . . . Dyker, no fool, would not try wholesale murder in the streets of Sentinel nor would he place himself in the open.

Dyker arose and came to the curb as Thoroughgood assisted Kristina to the ground. With a slight inclination of his head, he doffed his freshly blocked pearl-gray Stetson. He wore a perfectly tailored suit of black broad-cloth which didn't show a wrinkle. Even in this conservative garb, in spite of wilting heat and dust, he retained his easy, dapper elegance. His bench-made Justins were polished to a high gloss.

The deep grooves at the corners of his lips twitched in the faintest of smiles. "My new adversary? Well, Bob, something of a change for you, taking orders from a young lady."

Thoroughgood's mouth tightened with the unveiled gibe but he held temper, plainly determined not to betray the depth of the rancor existing here. "Miss Kristina Nilssen," he said shortly. "Santee Dyker . . ."

Dyker bowed over her hand. "My pleasure, Miss Nilssen. And yours — for you've won."

76

Kristina smiled, a little stiffly. "I do not want to crow, Mister Dyker. I'm sorry."

Dyker laughed softly. "Crow is what I'm eating, my dear; beak, claws, and feathers. With a side dish of humble pie . . . not for long, perhaps." His bland gaze found Channing. "Ah, the horseherd. Who would have suspected you'd retaliate with such a vengeance? You have Streak nursing a double grudge — as well as his shoulder. He's over at Dr. McGilway's now. And poor Whitey . . ." Dyker clucked his tongue.

"What is it? Did something happen yesterday?" Her voice was imperative.

Dyker chuckled. "'O what tangled webs we weave.' And so on, eh Bob?"

"Shut up, Santee!" Thoroughgood rasped. To Kristina he said urgently, "Sis, you don't understand —"

"But I was about to," she said icily. "You will please go on, Mister Dyker."

He told it all, half-smiling and without a shade of emotion, mentioning the brutality of his men to old Brock as dispassionately as Channing's killing of Whitey and wounding of Streak.

"Oh, terrible, terrible," she breathed. "I did not know . . ." She swung fiercely on Thoroughgood, her small fist striking him on the chest. "What kind of human wolf are you — all of you? Are you animals to tear each other to gorge yourselves on this land?"

"Figured you for more gumption, sis," Thoroughgood muttered.

"Gumption! Brawling and killing, this is to make men of you?" There was an almost hysterical

77

vehemence in her words that made Channing think, *It goes deeper than just this, with her. She's not the type to upset this bad. What could it be?* She abruptly calmed, saying with a despairing, quiet disgust, "I don't want the land. Not at this price. I will sign the ranch over to you wolves . . . tear it apart, and your Strip too. I don't want any of it!"

Old Brock spoke then, his cracked old voice laying its calm sanity on the tableau. "Don't stampede yet, Missy. Best tally the facts, see which way your stick floats. This child's an impartial observer, seems to it swings agin Santee. Shiloh here and Channin' staked their lives . . ."

She swung to face Channing, fists clenching at her sides as her eyes blazed at him. "Yes, you — *you killer!* Go away — stay out of my sight."

Channing's face paled under its deep weathering; swift and bewildered anger roiled in him and then he turned and strode away, walking fast. Shiloh clumped up beside him. "God's sake, boy. She didn't mean it, she wasn't thinkin'. Don't go off redheaded . . ."

"She meant it," Channing said low-voiced. "Don't get in my way, Shiloh."

He walked on and hardly knew when he turned in at Judd's saloon. He went to the bar and silently raised two fingers to the bald bartender. One look at his face relaxed Doc Willis' habitual scowl as he moved quickly to set out a glass and slosh it full. Then he went to the far end of the bar and seemed absorbed in a newspaper.

Channing stared into his glass without touching it. *Well, what now?* Already his rage was evaporating;

though he hated the self-admission, there remained little but the belated smarting of hurt feelings. Quite suddenly he felt like a damned fool. He'd prided himself on his ability to contain his emotions with a limit marked by independent pride, yet had flared up like a damp-eared schoolboy at this girl's condemnation. Thoroughgood and Shiloh would reason with Kristina Nilssen, bring her to her senses. Maybe . . . He picked up the drink and downed it. A stubborn reserve warmed in him with the liquor. The rest of his personal reaction might be foolish, but a man's wounded pride was no joke. She wasn't the begging kind, but neither was he . . . let her make the move.

The batwing doors parted and Santee Dyker sauntered to the bar a few feet away. "Whiskey, and none of your backbar swill . . . Well, friend, so that's the blow-up? How would you like to —"

"How would you like a dead nephew?" Channing cut in coldly.

Dyker's narrow shoulders shook with silent laughter. "Well, that's my answer. Certainly there's no deceit in you. You could have accepted my offer, then bided your time."

"Some of us are too dumb for you, Santee."

"Don't mistake me," Dyker said pleasantly, watching Doc fill his glass from a bottle under the bar. "I don't confuse honesty with stupidity." He sipped delicately, pale eyes remote and speculative. "Honesty is . . . shall we say, an untenable luxury for a man of my disposition."

"Along with self-respect, eh?"

Dyker smiled. "One man's tonic is another's poison, my friend. I'm a gambler, not merely with cards — with life. I needed new horizons, new challenges, when I left the Mississippi with a substantial fortune lining my pockets. The great cattle empires, modern baronies erected by men who risked all on a single gutty decision — what better does our fair land have to offer a gambler? I found this area remote and lawless enough, yet prosperous enough, for me to play the house according to my own rules. The Strip is the biggest stake of my lifetime, a key to wealth and power in cattle country. All I was afraid of was a dull game. Thoroughgood has courage and imagination, but his unfortunate scruples might have made him easy prey, if not for you." Santee Dyker raised his glass. "To you, my friend . . . for making the game interesting."

The brief fanatical intensity of him reminded Channing incongruously of his father. He felt no fear, but a cold unease that brought realization: in a way the man was crazy — with a dispassionate and unscrupled insanity that made him worse than any poor maniac who could not help himself. The elegant manners were a convenient façade. A woman, friendship, a full stomach, standards of right and wrong which a man could break and regret — the passions of ordinary men did not exist for Santee Dyker. Even the winner's stakes might well turn to ashes in his mouth, for only the challenge was his food and drink, and his bride, and his one friend, and when it was done, what could he have?

Both men faced around to the rear as the door of the back room opened. Anne LeCroix came out, nodded pleasantly to Channing. "Thought I heard your voice." To Santee she said coldly, "You're in Indian territory, aren't you? The Stockman's Bar handles the carriage trade."

Dyker set his glass down, smiling. "Partisanship, Annie? I'd give that a thought. I have a majority interest in the Sentinel Freighting Company now, you know. I can cut off your liquid supplies."

"You have the integrity of a rattlesnake, Santee," she said calmly.

"Good, I like spirited opposition. Channing here provided a bit, but he's bowing out. Too bad." Dyker tipped his hat and walked out.

Anne LeCroix came to the bar and crossed her arms on it. She shuddered faintly. "That cold-blooded little . . ." She looked at Channing narrowly. "You quit Spur? Why? And what did he mean?"

Channing shook his head. "No matter now."

"I've some good liquor in the office," she said abruptly. "Come along." She turned and walked back to the rear door, turned there and cocked her head with a quizzical smile. "Come now, I won't bite."

The yellow dog curled in the sawdust snarled as he passed it following Anne into the office. It was a narrow room furnished with a massive walnut desk and hand-carved armchairs. She walked to a highboy and stood on tiptoe to reach down a bottle and glasses. "Peach brandy. Judd — my husband — favored it."

Channing sat on the edge of a chair, balancing his hat on his knee with a sense of mounting embarrassment. He sensed that this cool and self-possessed woman did not extend an invitation lightly, and it made him wary. He accepted the glass she handed him, nodded his thanks. She leaned back in the other chair, crossing her legs and lightly swinging her free foot back and forth. In a land where women quickly faded, she looked younger than her age, full-bodied yet girlishly demure in a prim white shirtwaist and full blue skirt. From the window at her back sunlight built her shining hair to a red-gold corona. Only the faint, brittle lines around her eyes and mouth betrayed hard experience.

"A friendly bribe," she smiled, "for your confidence . . . After how you took Streak apart the other day, I expect Santee had good reason for his words. But there's more, isn't there?"

Channing relaxed a little. He gave her the sparest outline of yesterday's incidents. "Good," she said softly. "All Spur needed was a man who could meet that bunch on their own ground . . . But you've quit, why?"

"The girl doesn't like killers."

"Doesn't the little fool know the difference?"

"There's a difference?"

"You know there is — as in fighting fire with fire. But you're not really leaving?"

"What do you care?"

"I'd like to see you stay." Her eyes were wide and level — blue candor, like Kristina's. But this was no unworldly immigrant girl; Anne LeCroix's candor would mask a personal motive, and he wondered what it was. He watched her narrowly, unspeaking.

"Channing, you're no child. Neither am I. We've both seen life — perhaps more of it than we care to." Her voice held a warm and inviting hint, but he detected a brittle, calculating note. And then, remembering small things he had seen but taken little note of, he understood.

He said softly: "Thoroughgood?"

She drew a quick little breath, rose abruptly and went to the window; stared out at the dingy alley. Her tone was low and brittle. "Of course. It's that obvious? Well . . . that's right. How much of a fool can a woman be? Judd LeCroix took me out of an Albuquerque dive and married me. A love match on his part — it had to be, for he knew my past. He was a good man. I tried to make him a good wife. But he had to come to Sentinel and build this saloon. From the moment I saw Bob Thoroughgood —" She flung out her hand in a little futile gesture. "And I'd thought I'd had all romantic notions knocked out of me. That was four years ago; his wife was still alive, and so was Judd. Yet me, blushing like — a damned schoolgirl . . . and I haven't changed. That's what I mean. How much of a fool can a woman be!"

"Four years ago," he echoed. "No problem there."

"No?" The word was larded with bitter vehemence. "Why, he's in love with a memory first — then with his precious damned Spur. To him I'm a fixture around here — like Doc, or the bar." A faint flush mounted to her face. "I didn't mean to tell you any of this. All I started out to do was . . . persuade you to stay. Bob will fight Santee to the end, I know . . . and he might have a fighting chance to stay alive, with you."

He turned his hat in his hands, looking at it bleakly. "You can bottle things in too long."

"Are you talking to me — or yourself?"

"Just talking." He clamped his hat on, turned toward the door. She followed him and laid a hand on his arm. Her smile was genuine. "I was right. I liked you when I first saw you."

"Thanks."

"You don't talk much. You seem to think the more."

"A woman has a right to her feelings, same as men."

"But not many men think that way. And . . . you'll stay on with Spur?"

"That depends on Miss Nilssen." He added, almost reprovingly, "She's no fool."

"I see." Anne was smiling as she studied his face. "Well, I'm sorry; I have little cause to like women. The men respect me, they know I run a clean place. But their womenfolk are certain that any woman who runs a saloon is one of easy virtue."

"People talk and hens cackle. Morning, ma'am."

"Goodbye, Channing . . . and thank you."

He stepped outside and headed down the street for the business building. He hadn't covered half the distance when he saw Kristina Nilssen coming, holding her skirt a few inches above her quick pert steps. She came straight up to him, looking pale but determined.

"I am sorry, mister. I made a mistake."

Channing looked over her head to where Thorough-good and Shiloh leaned against the tie rail, watching them. Brock placidly waited on one of the saddle horses. Some perversity Channing couldn't help made him say thinly, "They must have made some fancy medicine."

Her head tilted defiantly back. "Listen, they talk me into nothing. I make up my own mind. I was mad, I think better. Now I want you back."

He simply nodded. She turned and marched back to the buggy. Thoroughgood swung her to the high seat, stepped up beside her with a frosty glance for Channing. "Deal's concluded, lease is signed and paid for." He added gruffly, "Glad you're stayin' on."

Brock leaned from horseback, extending Channing a horny hand. "*Adios,* hoss."

"Will you please change your mind and come home with us?" Kristina asked earnestly. "You're very welcome."

"Little lady, no. My stick floats upstream. To them mountains . . . Thankee for loan of the hoss. Be bringin' him in. See you all then."

Jogging back on the road to Spur, Thoroughgood was filled with boyish exuberance, full of his plans for the future. "Shiloh, you're going to El Paso . . ."

"Right this minute?" the *segundo* inquired dryly.

"Tomorrow. You're fetching us back a shorthorn herd."

"Your pet scheme, eh? You know the old man never bought it."

"How about you, sis?" Thoroughgood demanded. "You buying it?"

"Take care of the ranch is in your hands, mister. I'm just a dumb little squarehead, eh?"

Thoroughgood coughed embarrassedly. "Ahem . . . you'll be all right." He looked at her intently. "We'll lay this on the line. Santee isn't finished with us by a long shot. Got to be sure you're ready to buy that too. There'll be no turning back."

Channing saw a slow unhappiness shape her mouth; she'd learned something of life and men that morning, and the lesson was not a pleasant one. But her lips tightened. "No turning back," she said firmly.

CHAPTER
EIGHT

Streak Duryea was idly pleased that he'd once mastered the trick of building a cigarette one-handed. Expertly he shaped and sealed the quirly, closed his thin lips on it and snapped a match alight on his thumbnail. Exhaling with a grunted sigh, he leaned back on the blankets of his lower bunk, wincing as his bandage-swathed shoulder caught his weight.

Damn that brush jumper. For a gambler, Santee should have read the man more accurately. But Santee's very coldness sometimes blinded him to men's natures, as in thinking that force would bend Elwood Brock's mule-stubborn will. Despite his hatred for the mustanger, Streak felt a deep and grudging respect. The man had taken a savage whipping that should have broken body and spirit, yet less than twenty-four hours later had sought out the man who'd administered it, beaten him to a pulp with three of his men present. That impressed Streak far more than Channing's rescue of Brock; the first time Channing had been a man alone in strange country, throwing back defiance in the teeth of Anchor Ranch and all its power. Nobody but a fool kicked at an angry rattler; yet Channing was no fool, and Streak wondered what drove the man . . .

Lying on his back with the murmurs of the card players in his ears, the rest of the men sprawled in their bunks, Streak turned his head, squinting against the bite of smoke. The bunkhouse was twenty by forty, partitioned for warmth against the high-country chill, with its five sets of double bunks, its battered chairs and settee and the table in the center littered with yellowed, page-curling magazines and an omnipresent Dutch Almanac, and the potbellied stove crackling its warmth through the stale atmosphere. It was like a hundred bunkhouses Streak Duryea had known since his orphaned boyhood, where men came and went, froze and sweated for thirty and found, bare of luxury and shorn to a minimum of comfort.

But there was a difference. The floor here was caked with filth and carelessly strewn with gear, the walls grimy and soot-smudged, violating the working puncher's law of scrupulous cleanliness in his one abode. Streak looked at these men, his mouth twisted. Trash, all of them; the dregs of the chuckline who drifted because no decent place could long absorb their ilk, replacing every honest Anchor man because Santee Dyker had a dirty job in prospect.

And he ramrodded this scum . . . Streak Duryea felt an abrupt backwash of contempt. Maybe part of Channing's unexpected reaction was a savage capacity for anger against injustice. For Streak himself, lacking the capacity, Channing's way was too unpredictable. He sucked his cigarette, sighting down its glowing tip. A man guided by his own self-sufficient standards had an inner toughness, a drive behind him that would override a man of purposeless cynicism. Where, how, had Duryea lost his youthful lodestar? Too much knocking around in the worst quarters when he'd still had a choice, this leading to one self-compromise after another till there was nothing left to compromise. Savagely he ground out the cigarette. The hell with it. This was his berth, housed with the prideless scum whose wild and violent way of life he'd chosen . . .

The droned murmurs of the card players had sharpened with an ugly note that caused Streak to raise himself on one elbow. Ward Costello was playing stud with Arnt Chance, a spare, hard-bitten man of forty. Bee Withers straddled the bench by Costello, watching with his foolish grin, the half-healed cuts on his face a sickly color in the sallow lamplight.

Chance set his palms on the table, pushing stiffly to his feet. His ax-slash of a mouth was tight. "Like to see you deal that over," he said softly. "Don't usually git fancy belly strippers this far away from the big towns, big casinos."

Costello's slender hands did not move on the table. "You can go to hell, my man," he stated evenly. "Your deck. You dealt the hand — and shot me an ace."

Chance's lean arm snaked across the table, suddenly snatching Costello's right wrist and twisting it viciously. Costello's hand opened spasmodically. A card fell from it. "Figured so," Chance said thickly. "Ace was up your sleeve. Switched this three for it."

He released Costello's wrist and stepped quickly back. At the same time Bee Withers stood, a high, gangly shadow behind Costello. Bee settled his colorless stare on Arnt Chance, and was motionless, waiting. Streak reached to the gunbelt pegged on the wall by his hand, lifting his Colt from holster. The sound of its cocking broke the smoke-hung quiet.

"Sit down, Withers," he said quietly. "You too, Arnt."

Arnt Chance wavered for a feisty moment, then growled, "Ahhh," disgustedly as he swung toward his bunk. Withers remained as he was, watching Arnt. Costello, scowling as he rubbed his wrist, spoke sharply. Withers slacked casually back to the bench.

Setting his teeth against the pain, Streak swung his legs off the bunk and hunched his narrow shanks to a sitting position. "You're here on sufferance, nephew. Don't prod your luck."

Costello shrugged, picked up the deck and riffled it. His indifference smarted, goading Streak to anger. The men were all watching; two defeats at Channing's hands had already lessened his stature, a loss of face he could not afford. "Goddamn you, Costello, look at me when I talk to you."

Costello gave him a sullen glance. "I don't take your orders."

"Not you, not Santee's coddled nephew," Streak jeered. "But you'll damned well hear me say what we all know. You and your heel dog are laying in here because one man curled your tail. You haven't got the guts to jump reservation while he's inside a hundred miles. One man."

"That's right," murmured Costello. "Took you down a peg or so, though, didn't he?"

Streak leaned forward, lamplight flaring hot and wicked against his eyes. "He did, by God. And I'll kill him for it!"

"Trouble, Streak?"

Santee had opened the door and was lounging against the jamb. His casual query bore the texture of bland steel.

Streak let his breath out. "No trouble."

"Do you take me for a blind man or a fool? Come up to the house. Now. You too, Ward — and Withers."

Streak arose and sidled painfully around the table, preceding Costello and Withers through the doorway. Santee moved stonily aside to let them pass. Streak tramped slowly up the dark slope, cradling his calico-slung right arm in his left hand. The still-green logs of the house oozed pitch, a pungent pine scent carried to Streak's nostrils by a chill wind dipping off the peaks. He shivered. Behind, he heard Costello's quick, nervous breathing. Santee was on the peck and no mistake. The ice-veined little bastard carried no gun, duded himself up and talked like a book read, but foul-mouthed hardcases twice his size talked soft and walked easy around Santee Dyker. Streak, for all his aloof cynic's pride, knuckled under to Santee without shame.

Streak stepped into the front room, shifting his feet uneasily on the deep grass-green carpet. The room was small but impeccably furnished. The fragile-looking furniture, of some tropical wood Streak couldn't identify, had been freighted in; it was perfectly congruous to Santee's casual taste. His fat Mexican housekeeper was kneeling by the brick fireplace, poking at a blazing log. "*Vamos, andale,*" Santee said curtly. The woman heaved to her feet, shuffled to the silver coffee service on a low tabaret, picked it up and vanished down a corridor, her *guaraches* slap-slapping the floor.

Santee walked to the highboy and spilled some cognac from a cut-glass decanter into a glass. He walked to the divan, sat and gently swirled the dark liquor. "Now, I am not going to mince words with you, Ward," he said in the casually dispassionate manner that Streak recognized as masking his wickedest moods. "This is the third time in a week there's been trouble on your account. Didn't I tell you last time — no more poker with the men?"

"A man needs diversion," Ward said tonelessly. "If they want to play —"

"You have to cold-deck."

"Their idea. Let them prove it."

"Arnt caught him in the act tonight," Duryea broke in mildly. "Had an ace in his sleeve."

Santee exhaled gently. "I see." He let the silence run on till Costello began to fidget. "Ward," he said finally, "just what the hell am I going to do with you? You're no damned use on-range with that lily skin and soft body. Can't handle a gun except for that trick sleeve-rig; you'd crack like rotten ice in a real clinch. You're damned close to it already, afraid he'll come here — pot you from ambush. You're afraid to leave the ranch, building your real danger out of proportion. Hanging here like Old Man Trouble himself, getting bored, getting in my way, fleecing my crew —"

"No call to talk that way," Costello muttered.

Santee slammed down his glass on the tabaret, sloshing the contents across its varnished top. "Who has a better right?" He swung to his feet, made a turn around the divan, hands rammed in his waistcoat pockets. He halted in front of Costello. "You're a miserable excuse even for a tinhorn," he said contemptuously. "At this moment I'd need very damned little to have you escorted to Spur and turned over to . . . your friend."

Costello paled swiftly, but wisely held his tongue.

"There was one person I cared for," Santee went on softly. "You're tolerated here for her sake, that alone. I'm sick of the sight of you. Understand? You can't stay here forever, jumping at every sound or shadow. Sooner or later you'll have to face him or run. What are you going to do?"

Costello's hand rubbed his throat; he swallowed, managed a low, miserable, "I don't know."

Streak had seated himself gingerly on a fragile chair, watching this with speculative amusement. Santee had once told him that when he'd worked the riverboat gambling tables, his sister, a regally beautiful woman whom Streak gathered had been as cold and distant as Santee himself, had shilled for him. Her armor has been penetrated only once — by some weasely little drummer named Costello who'd left her with an illegitimate child. After she'd died of consumption, exacting a dying promise, Santee had raised the boy on the riverboats. Young Ward's weak and vacillating nature had been easily molded by early environs — gambling and a transient existence.

Afterward, like a bad penny, he'd turn up occasionally in Santee's vicinity with Bee Withers in tow like a patient dog. The partnership between Ward and Bee, ill-assorted except that neither was any damned good, was perfectly complemented. Ward had no spine, but enough impassioned gambler's gall to maintain them both; Bee was too stupid to be afraid, but responded quickly and efficiently to trouble, handling Costello's difficulties. When the game turned against him, he'd return to loaf off his uncle's bounty for a time, and be off again.

Now Santee was plainly fed up. Duryea almost chuckled aloud, waiting with relish for the rancher's next words. Surprised when Santee curtly addressed Withers: "Bee, you ran with some of the toughest hardcases in Arizona before you partnered up with Ward, didn't you?"

Withers gave a guarded nod.

"Now you've seen this Channing on the shoot, how would you rate him?"

"Right pert, Mister Dyker." Bee's voice was a broken mumble through his wired-up jaws.

"All right, think. You've seen the best of them, who would you pick to face him in a stand-up?"

"Feller from my home-place in the Tennessee hills," Withers mumbled unhesitatingly. "Feller named Landers. We called him 'Brace.' Grease lightnin', dead shot. Gun was a third hand to Brace, Mister Dyker."

"All right, all right," Santee motioned impatiently. "Where is he now?"

"Last seen him five years ago, we was runnin' with the Hashknife outfit in the Tonto Rim country. Of recent years he's hung purty close over Prescott way."

"Would a letter reach him there?"

Withers scratched his tow thatch. "Raickon so. But he'll come mighty high . . ."

"Write him, let me worry about the rest."

"Cain't write, Mister Dyker."

Santee sighed profoundly. "I'll write him, you add your mark." He swung to Costello. "When Channing's finished, you clear out. For good. Get to your room now, don't let me hear of you around the bunkhouse again."

Flushed with humiliation, Costello walked from the room with Withers shambling behind. Santee leisurely drew a twisted cheroot from his breast pocket, clipped the end with a gold cutter on his watch chain, and lighted it.

"Why a special man?" Streak asked. "I could deadfall him straightaway enough."

"As you did Custis Thursday, yes," Santee said musingly, his eyes lambent through the swirling smoke. "Ambushing Thursday was a job of necessity, not of passion, with you. You might be a trifle overeager with Channing, nor is he an old man to be taken unawares even in the dead of night. It must have been he, not that bumbling old Spur *segundo,* who trailed you from Brock's cabin. He's Spur's ace-in-the-hole, a man who's been in this kind of fight before and understands it. And has an uncommon knack of doing the unexpected, what in another would be stupidity or insanity. A successful gambler knows when to cut the odds; having Channing cut down in a stand-up encounter would be certain and impressive. He's the opposition's morale. As Napoleon said, 'In war, the morale is to the physical as three to one' . . . Meanwhile, there's this herd Thoroughgood is having shipped from El Paso."

Streak nodded moodily. Earlier that day, at Santee's order, he'd dispatched a rider to town to listen to the saloon grapevine. "Yeah. Shiloh Dawes and part of the Spur crew left on the train today, was the talk in town. Ought to be back in a couple weeks."

"The girl must have come here with capital," Santee mused. "Spur was down to a shoestring from old Thursday's clumsy extravagance. I never thought they could pay Brock's price, let alone re-stock their range. They couldn't have much left. If that herd were wiped out . . ."

"That's half the trouble," Streak observed. "Word's that John Straker and Spur might mend their differences."

"Ah?" Santee said sharply. "You didn't mention that earlier."

"Just talk, Elam said. He overheard one of Straker's crew tell the barber that the Nilssen girl and Thoroughgood were over at Mexican Bit yesterday. They talked with Straker for quite a spell."

"A mutual protection league — against us?" Santee released his breath sibilantly, smiling frostily. "Just possible, yes . . . and a shrewd move. Have Elam keep his ears open; when we know their next move — we move."

CHAPTER
NINE

The men stood uneasily around the parlor, holding glasses of barely tasted whiskey. All were dressed for the occasion. Thoroughgood looked strangely at ease in his black broadcloth, but his near-perpetual scowl had scarcely relaxed. Channing squirmed his shoulders uncomfortably in a suit borrowed from a bunkie, the cravat and choker collar giving him an acute sense of suffocation.

The two visitors shared their hosts' half-awkward, half-hostile silence. The master of Mexican Bit was a towering, lean man, straight as a rifle barrel, looking the military careerist he'd been. At fifty John Straker's hair was a smooth, dead-white cap which, with precisely trimmed mustaches and brittle gray eyes, gave him a look of steel-willed distinction. He wore a handsome Prince Albert over his ruffled white shirt with string tie. His foreman, Mel Daley, was a quiet-eyed, taciturn man with a long horse face. He rolled a tobacco cut in the pocket of his cheek, and the front of his slightly rumpled and age-rusty suit was already stained by it.

"Come to table," Kristina called from the dining room. The men began a concerted shuffle through the dividing archway. Channing was the last to enter; like the others, he came stock-still to stare at her. He knew she'd spent many hours cutting and sewing on some rich material she'd purchased in town, readying the dress she wore. It was of blue watered silk, low-cut from the milky smoothness of neck and shoulders, bodice hugging her upper body and skirt belling prettily. She had done her hair differently, gathered smoothly atop her small head in a way at once Eastern and alien, yet admirable. Still none of her handsome freshness was lost, rather now taking a man's eye with a soft radiance.

Speaking in her soft, strong accent she directed them to chairs. Channing's eye went over the table with mounting amazement. The fine linen tablecloth and silverware and matched china must have belonged to Thoroughgood's wife, but the quantity of food — enough for a Scandinavian banquet — had been prepared under Kristina's direction, with the unwillingly pressed help of the ranch cook. He recognized several Swedish dishes — *knakkebrod, getmesost,* and little rosette fried cakes filled with jam. At each plate was a small glass of mild-appearing liquid.

Kristina took her place at the head of the table with John Straker on her right gallantly stepping up to hold her chair. The men stiffly seated themselves. She smilingly raised her glass. "Gentlemen . . . ?"

Mel Daley lifted his drink suspiciously, giving her his mournful glance. "What you call this snifter, ma'am?"

"*Glogg.* I think you call it — punch?"

Daley's drooping roan mustaches stirred in a grin tolerant of female fooferaw; he took the drink in a lusty swallow. For a moment he was motionless, but swallowing hard. "By the Sam Hill," he muttered. Kristina laughed heartily. John Straker held a stern face, raising his glass with a respectful, "Your very good health, ma'am," and now with the potent concoction warming their stomachs the atmosphere thawed.

Kristina took little food herself but chatted animatedly as she passed dishes, urging them to sample each. Channing ate in silence, knowing his presence here was by token only, a morale backing to the proposition Kristina had discussed with Thoroughgood and himself yesterday. She had climaxed her visit to Mexican Bit by inviting Straker and his foreman to supper and they were to play their parts. The stage was well-set, Channing conceded with a faint cynicism. All very neat, very charming. By contrast to Kristina Nilssen's usual candor, this was an elaborate background for her purpose; he found it disquieting. Certainly Kristina was no woman of the world like Anne LeCroix, but maybe a woman knew these things by instinct. This girl's appearance of childish naïveté was deceptive, though not intentionally so; she assessed a situation with a native shrewdness that made up for ignorance. She had stepped smoothly into the reins of Spur ownership from the first, and by now was imperceptibly guiding some of Thoroughgood's own hard-gained lifetime experience. Channing refilled his glass from the punchbowl, dourly thinking, *Well, she knows what she wants, more than you can say.* But through the thought was threaded a nagging sense of disappointment

99

She laughingly scolded Mel Daley for protesting a third helping of *knakkebrod,* then turned to John Straker. The fitful lamplight played restless highlights on her hair as she leaned her chin on her hand, lips tilted pixie-like. "You are a cold businessman, Mr. Straker, no friv — frivolity, eh?"

Straker patted his lips with his napkin, saying hastily, "I am enjoying every minute, ma'am. An old bachelor never realizes his barren existence except from a delightful contrast."

Her laugh tinkled scoffingly. "Why Mr. Straker, you're a mighty fine figure of a man . . . and old?"

Only old enough to be her father, Channing thought and took a drink that balled in his stomach with a sour heat.

"That is far better," Kristina murmured serenely. "And . . ." *And now to business,* Channing thought, recognizing the subtle altering of her expression to mulish determination.

Kristina outlined her intention casually, deferring modestly to Thoroughgood now and then by asking him to detail several points. It would involve the throwing together of the crews, wagons and gear of Spur and Mexican Bit to move the shorthorn herd, which Shiloh Dawes was now bringing from El Paso, onto the Strip. Neither Spur's mistress nor its foreman tried to garnish the fact that this was a protective measure. Thoroughgood anticipated that Santee Dyker would strike at that herd, which represented Spur's big experimental gamble for future prosperity. Without it, the real advantage of Spur's holding the coveted graze was nil. The stringy, half-wild beeves which already constituted the stock of Spur's waning fortunes could be grazed on its range proper with no loss. Santee would be wary of taking on the combined crews of his two rivals, particularly if they posed a powerful retaliatory force. Kristina wanted to avoid bloodshed at all cost, and armed strength was the deterrent she meant to use. Channing felt renewed approbation; there was no shame to her determined refusal to further her ambition at the cost of men's lives.

Straker nodded attentively. "And my stake in this, ma'am?"

She explained that Spur would share the Strip within an arbitrary limit of the number of head that Mexican Bit could graze there at any one time, for a two-year period. Elwood Brock's agreement to this arrangement had already been secured, and she made it clear that after Mexican Bit had helped safely disperse the shorthorns over the graze, Straker's only commitment was to come to Spur's aid in any emergency arising from Santee Dyker's antagonism during those two years. If Straker was satisfied with its conditions, she would dispatch a rider tomorrow to Anchor with a note informing Santee Dyker of the details of their agreement, an oblique warning.

"Hum," Straker murmured, seeming to turn it in his mind; he was quickly decided. "A handshake is considered sufficient in these matters." Kristina did not hide her radiant delight, as, bowing over her hand, he added with a wry gallantry, "Young lady, I've been trapped before, but never so charmingly."

The relief of slacked tension was plain. Thoroughgood unbent so far as to lay a hand on Straker's shoulder when they left the table for the parlor, saying, "John, we've been a sorry pair of mossyhorns not to see it out this way before."

Straker chuckled. "No pretty middleman before . . ."

Kristina served coffee, and for an hour she was the gay hostess, no longer in a role. Then Straker stood and reached for his hat "Thank you for the excellent supper, ma'am," he said, adding forcefully: "I'll call again."

Kristina stood on the porch and watched Straker and Daley ride from the ranch yard, soon lost beyond the long, crooked shadows thrown by the lamplight from parlor windows. Then she turned, wrinkling her nose at Thoroughgood who was lounging in the doorway. "He is a funny old man. But a gentleman."

"See here, sis," Thoroughgood said gravely, "there's a thing or so you should get straight."

"Oh?"

"Wouldn't say you meant to trifle exactly, but he took it seriously. Want to watch you don't stir up another hornet's nest."

She picked up her skirts and stepped past him to enter, saying stiffly, "It was yust an arrangement of business."

"Sure, sure," the foreman said seriously. "But you're a young and pretty woman. Use that fact on a man to get your wants, you'll find he won't stop where you draw the line." He nodded abruptly, said "Good night," and left for the bunkhouse.

102

Channing finished his third cup of coffee, scalded his tongue in his haste, and started to stand quickly.

"Channing!" She turned to face him with a rustle of skirts, a small frown marring her brow. "Channing, it is true, eh? What he says?"

She was standing close before him, and he sank back on the divan. "Guess so," he said uncomfortably.

Her smile was speculative as she sat beside him, drawing her skirts close. "I am pretty, then?"

He could smell a faint sachet from her skin, and the lamplight laid an ivory sheen on her shoulders. His face felt hot, the high collar choking. "I'd better —"

"Have some coffee!" She bent forward to fill his cup. Looking at the back of her head, his embarrassment ebbed. She was, after all, competent mistress of Spur or no, a young girl in a new party gown, probably the first she'd owned . . . gala finery worn for the eyes of an aging rancher and two not-young foremen. And there was him . . . a killer near her age, he thought with cold self-castigation. With a faint pity, too, and an akin understanding.

"I'll have that coffee," he said quietly. Their eyes met as she handed him the cup; she flushed slowly. "Thank you," she said low-voiced.

After a moment's silence, he said: "You got it all now. Everything you want."

"Oh," she said softly, looking away. "You see plainly. I am greedy, eh? That's not being a very good woman, I suppose . . ."

He started to protest, but she shook her head. "No, it is true." She looked down at her skirt, pleating the crisp folds caressingly between her fingers. "This ordering of men's affairs, it's nice to be able to do. But Bob was right, he says I am not fair. And I don't feel so good, hearing it put that way." She turned her head suddenly, her words a vehement outpouring.

"It is not so easy to be fair! My father came to this country to find a good life. The first year on his farm it was corn and potatoes. A drought came and the sun scorched it all. The second year he sowed wheat. Now locusts like a plague of Jehovah ate away the farmlands. So neighbors, they quit and said it was no good. But Papa tried again. He worked in the lumber camps each winter to support his wife and children and buy seed to try again. He planted more wheat It was good this time; good rains, and no locusts. Standing tall like gold in the sun. A week before the cutting . . ."

A dry sob broke in her throat. He wanted to stop her, but she went on. Hail had flattened the wheat. Her father had come in from the ruin of his fields to find his wife Sigrid in labor and terrible pain. He had gone to the nearby town for a doctor. And had found the settlement deserted, save for one old man. Some young Sioux braves had gotten hold of whiskey and murdered a farm family nearby. The farmer's wife had escaped to tell the settlement. The panicked citizens had fled south to a larger town. It was as though her father's brain had snapped at the news. Without a word, he'd rushed off into the empty night. The next morning the old man had gone to the Nilssen farm. Sigrid and her unborn child must have died before her husband had returned. In their bed the old man had found Kristina's two little sisters, their throats cut. Eric Nilssen lay dead on the floor, his wrists slashed by the same knife.

Kristina pressed her hands to her temples, her eyes shining and hard. "I was working in St. Paul . . . did not know till I came home for a visit a month later. The old man told me. So I have everything now, everything —"

She broke down, and Channing, like a sensible man, put his arms around her and let her sob like a child against his shoulder. He said gently: "A sight too much remembering. Better to let it go."

She drew away, her tear-stained face serious and abruptly calm. "You know why I hate this useless death, this killing?"

He said humbly, "Didn't before."

"And you have killed," she murmured with no censure to it. "You're not that way, you have kindness. Why, Channing?"

"There's enough hurt for one evening."

"Tell me."

Channing's tongue was sluggish, blurring the words. But her story had shaken him and now he wanted to talk. Wanted to tell her of his father with his Bible and birching rod.

"Your papa was a minister?"

"A deacon or elder in the church, when he was younger. Before Mom died. Heard folks say it was after that he got hard. I was too young to remember anything 'cept being raised by hand. The old man didn't go to church in my recall. Said it was a place for weaklings who had to be told the Word when it was all in the

105

Book, the way a man must live. I'll say this: if he took his own meaning from the Scriptures, he lived up to it."

"There was no word in his Bible of forgiveness, of love?"

"He missed nothing. Forgave the weak fools of the world and showed his love for his boy by raising him in — righteousness. He was a righteousness one, the old man. He hated guns most. Devil's tools for weak, wicked people to lean on . . . can't say he was wrong, can you?"

She didn't reply, her lips slightly parted as she watched his face.

Channing tugged at his collar with a finger, moved restlessly. "Well, I fooled once with a gun belonging to my uncle, shot it off by accident. The old man laid it on, worst he ever had, left me layin' like raw beefsteak. Uncle took me to a doctor, left me there. When the old man came nosin', the doc come out with a shotgun, swore he'd blow him to blazes if he set foot on the porch."

He'd been thirteen then. A scrawny kid with most of the hide flayed from his back. It had been nearly a month before he could leave his bed, the doctor's wife nursing him the while. The old man finally had recourse to the law and got a court order for the return of his son. The doctor swore he'd fight it. Rather than embroil the kindly couple further, young Channing had left in the dead of night. For the next week he'd put distance between himself and the town of his birth. He lived off berries and like truck till he came to a ranch where he was fed and given a charity job of swamping for the cook.

He'd saved his first meager earnings till he had enough to buy a second-hand Colt and ammunition. It became a ritualistic obsession to stand off in a draw away from the ranch, and, pretending that an old stump was his father's face, blaze coolly away at it. When the scars on his back were fully healed, his bitter hatred had relaxed. But the gun had become proficient habit, deadly habit that made a skinny, undersized kid stand head and shoulders with the biggest man. Backed by a savage vow that he'd be tormented no more.

The ranch crew had laughed, but not too loudly; something in his look softened their taunts. It wasn't till a Saturday night in town that a likkered cowhand strange to him had knocked him down for no better reason than it galled him to see a snot-nosed runt packing a man's weapon. Shaking with rage, young Ed Channing had called him out, let him pull his gun before the kid's smooth draw and speedy bullet sent him kicking in the street The man had lived for two days. When the news of his death came to Channing's boss, the white-haired rancher's comment had been grim and short: "You're a killer, boy. Get off my place."

Eleven years ago. Channing wasn't sure, but guessed that the drifting afterward and the nursing of the new, raw bitterness had really marked him so it showed. No one taunted him again; men gave him one look and a wide berth. He got used to men's cold scrutinies and their curt, "Sorry, no work here." But the railroads were building spur lines out of Kansas; troubleshooters were what they wanted, and he had no choice. The federal government had endowed the railroad with every alternate section of land along their siding, and the squatters had to be moved off. The pay was choice — if you could forget the shamed fright of half-starved hoe-grubbers you shoved back, the loathing in the eyes of their women, the scared cringing of ragged children. But Channing could not forget; when he moved on, it was far north, clear to Montana.

There had been work for a changed man, a brooding and silent stranger who stepped far aside to avoid trouble. But aimless driftings brought only small disappointments that piled up and dogged a man till he came to realize that if he found no meaning in life, he must make his own meaning. His crystallizing purpose sparked by the warmth of his first friendship — with Lacey Trobridge — had been the puncher's eternal dream, a ranch of his own — in partnership with his friend. Then he told the rest: the purpose destroyed, nothing to renew his purpose but revenge.

"Why," Kristina said softly, wonderingly, "you have never had anything! That's terrible . . ."

"Just life. It goes that way."

His words were almost indifferently matter-of-fact. Yet he was aware of an inward lightening, wondered now if something had left his system like a drained-off poison. Looking at the girl he saw her pale and shaken; the completeness of their cross-shared confidence left him uneasy, a little ashamed.

He gave an abrupt good night as be stood and quickly strode from the house. Once only and softly, she called his name; he didn't look back.

Nearing the bunkhouse he saw the cherry-glow of a cigar and the looming shadow of Thoroughgood leaning against the front wall. The foreman stepped out to plant his bulk solidly before the younger man. Channing halted, hearing his angry exhalation that made the cigar's coal flare redly against his frowning features. At the edge of speech, he relaxed with a faint shrug. "Guess you know."

"My place?" Channing murmured.

"Forget it." Thoroughgood dropped the cigar and ground it under his heel, adding with an acrid pointedness: "I've got to know you, like you, boy. Don't crowd that fact. Let's turn in."

CHAPTER
TEN

Two weeks later Kristina rode out to the branding grounds several miles west of Spur headquarters. The El Paso train with its line of cattle cars had jolted onto the siding at Sentinel late last night. Shiloh Dawes, dirty, tired and whiskered, had brought in the news. Thoroughgood had roused out the crew and had dispatched a rider to notify John Straker. Long before false dawn, the joint Spur-Anchor crews were unloading the shorthorns, starting the drive to the Spur range for the branding prior to the drive up the rugged plateau trails to the Strip.

Kristina capably reined in the buckboard a few yards beyond the branding fires where Thoroughgood and John Straker stood. Men were slapping hot iron on the hip of a bawling whiteface, tied and thrown on the scuffed earth. Kristina sat for a wide-eyed moment; her eyes stung and she coughed as furling smoke shifted on a hot current of air. Straker turned and saw her. He came to the buck-board and assisted her from the high seat, taking in with approval her calico shirt and leather riding skirt.

"Didn't hear you come, for the noise. What do you think of it?"

She made a wry face. "Looks painful."

His grin broadened. "To save more pain in the long run. Even then, a haired-over brand at roundup can come close to a bloody argument."

She nodded perfunctorily, her smile an absent one, eyes roving over the milling, dust-moiling herd, the cowboys cutting and bulldogging, a ritual panorama which another time would have held her breathless. She couldn't see Channing. She caught herself abruptly, angry at her un-bidden anxiety. Yet her honest reason for coming was to see him — speak to him, she corrected herself. If only to analyze for her own satisfaction the disturbing bond she'd felt between them since that night nearly two weeks ago.

Thoroughgood stepped over, giving her his curt working nod. "It's humming along, sis. With two crews and no hitches, we ought to be on the Strip in a few days."

"That's good." She glanced up at him, hands on her hips. "But Mister Dyker?"

"Mister Dyker knows," Thoroughgood said heavily. "A couple of his boys were hanging around at the depot last night. Likely he has a hardcase or two spotting us from the hills now."

"And?" she prompted anxiously.

Thoroughgood pinched his lower lip. "Anyone's guess. He'll know we got more men than him, that they're armed to the teeth, that there'll be a triple guard on the herd every night, that we ride flankers by day and night."

"They would try to shoot up our herd?"

"No-o," Straker said judiciously. "Stampede them, is our guess. They're not about to ride into our teeth, they'd be chewed and spit out in short order. But a noisy attack well-timed could spook the beeves so they'd not stop till they dropped. If they got pointed for badlands broke up by canyons or *malpais* — these fat stump-legged pets of Bob's would get busted to pieces."

Thoroughgood gave him a grim side-glance. "That's why the flanking scouts, sis. Eyes like Channing's on the lookout, holding our drive to wide-open country, nobody'll edge near enough to start anything."

"It's good they do not," she said gravely. "There are many lives here, men and animals, and money will not buy them back . . . Channing is on the scout?"

Thoroughgood's lean features sharpened; he opened his mouth, closed it, cleared his throat and said meagerly, "Yeah. South flank. A hundred yards out."

That is not what he meant to say, Kristina thought, and knew a sudden anger. It was none of his business. He thought she was a befuddled child, and she would show him what she thought Without speaking she swung back to her rig, mounted to the seat and took up the reins. Putting the team in motion, she did not look back.

She guided the wagon over the turf-clumped rolling ground in a wide skirt of the herd, rebelliously urging the team to a pace that threatened to creak the jolting buck-board apart. Seeing a rider sitting his horse in motionless isolation, she headed that way. She recognized him well before she reined the team to a halt that shrouded the parched ground in tan dust. She had not expected the unbidden excitement that now sparked her; she had half-expected his sullen withdrawal. Yet he looked wholly at ease, a cigarette between his sunburnt lips and one leg slung over his pommel. His nod and comment were pleasant if taciturn: "Hot day to push a team that hard."

She frowned slightly at this stolid contentment of a solitary man. *He likes being alone,* she thought, and her tumultuous mood honed her voice with gentle acid: "I would hate it to bother you, mister."

"Not the least bother," Channing said easily, but the uneasiness mounting in his face gave her satisfaction. She altered her approach to friendly intimacy. "I have seen that you avoid me."

He ground the cigarette out on his boot with a self-conscious downward scowl. "Not aware of it."

"Oh yes. When you see me coming, you find suddenly work to busy you. This, after walking out on me after the party — and talk."

His eyes went opaque and remote. "Nothing else to say. There's a thing about talk — can't be stopped once it starts. And that's no good."

"It is wrong — for friends to talk? This foolish line between bunkhouse and the owner — or maybe it's Thoroughgood you're afraid of."

"Not one or the other. No rule, no man alive, tells me my way."

"Then what?"

"You didn't see Bob's meaning," he said patiently. "He sees what I do. Drop it there."

"No." A strong undercurrent of emotion shaded her voice, and she felt no shame in it

"All right." He looked at the dead cigarette and tossed it away. He said tiredly: "A man like me's no good to anything touching him. Thoroughgood can tell that without knowing what you know."

"Why, I think he comes to like you now."

"Nothing to do with this other. Look . . . Kristina. You're young. Your life's ahead of you. Mine's about finished. Not in years, in the way I've lived them. The things I told you, the reason I'm here. To you it tallies to something romantic-seemin'."

Is that what you think? she thought with, a wondering pity, but held silence in the pause, and he went on: "To Bob and me, it adds to a bullet in the back. Or in the front, sooner or later, don't matter." His voice abruptly roughened. "You're not a fool; don't act one. Keep your distance. Maybe you understand that?"

A hurt anger flared out of her first emotion. She sputtered a Swedish expletive and reined the team into violent motion. She hauled in well away from him. Her face felt burning. *He did not mean that. He meant it for my good,* she thought. *If they are wrong, these thoughts, it will have to be.* She let her mouth tilt in a stubborn and speculative smile.

CHAPTER
ELEVEN

The fires of the camp made lone and ruddy beacons in the night's oceanic murk. Each man wolfing his supper in silence felt the communicated knife-edge of unease. The branding had been completed yesterday, and the drive to the Strip had begun that morning. The size of the herd and the progressive roughness of the terrain had held twenty men of the combined crews to a plodding pace. They expected to strike into the Strip lowlands late tomorrow and begin the job of dispersing the shorthorns safely across its immense, open-rolling acreage.

Now bivouacked for this last night on a semi-arid highland meadow which would accommodate the herd bed-grounds a quarter mile away, they all were of the same thought: that if Anchor struck at the herd, it must be tonight. The knowledge marked even John Straker's stern-held face where he sat by Thoroughgood on the tree of the chuckwagon. The Spur foreman forked the food around his tin plate in a bare pretense of eating. The cowhands around the fire ate stolidly if with little stomach; each would be serving long wary hours on a double guard which Thoroughgood had split into two shifts.

Channing, scheduled on the second shift at midnight, scraped up his plate and downed his coffee and was the first to head for his blankets beyond the drawn-up wagons. In a minute Shiloh Dawes unrolled his sugans and stretched out a yard away.

"Shiloh — how'll it come?"

"Law, son," the *segundo* whispered, "got to be a snake with brains to read Santee. *Quién sabe?* The dark could cover whatever he tries. That moon's a sliver, cat couldn't see much a paw away."

"Was thinking," Channing said sleepily, "about the scouts, out there alone. Stranger making to be one of us could ride close, ask one of 'em for a smoke maybe, and —"

A clatter of tinware by the tailgate of the chuckwagon broke him off. Both he and Shiloh came erect in their blankets. In the firelight stood a lean, gangling Spur puncher who'd broken the thick stillness by dropping his plate and cup resoundingly into the wreck pan. The squat figure of the cook faced him truculently. "What the hell was that for!"

"Sawmthin' to drag you awake, gutcheatuh," the puncher said in a long-drawn nasal drawl. "Thet gawd-damn grub's too turrible even for your makin'."

Several men chuckled. Tenseness relaxed like an unclosing fist Shiloh chuckled, settled back in his blankets. "We all needed that Let's get shut-eye."

Channing folded his arm under his head. He lay staring at the white star-blaze on a cobalt canopy of sky, tired to where his thoughts raveled into meaninglessness. Thoroughgood had pushed hard these last days, with time for but snatched hours of sleep. Channing tried to sort out his troubled thoughts . . . regretting his rough last words to Kristina and knowing he wouldn't take them back if he could. It remained as he'd told her and her romantic notions must stem from the disturbing confidences they had shared only once. Cut it clean, forget it, get some sleep. And he slept, his last thought of an empty sense of loss deeper than anything he had known.

He was awakened at midnight by somebody shaking him by the shoulder. He stumbled sleep-drugged from his blankets and moved over to his ground-hitched horse. Shiloh yawned broadly as he swung into leather, a stumpy, half-seen figure in the darkness. The five other riders constituting the shift relief fell in behind as they crossed the flat, bunch-grassed meadow toward the faintly stirring hulk of the herd, held in the rolling open according to plan.

A cold highland breeze trailing across Channing's face pulled him to chilled alertness. He buttoned his jumper to the collar and slacked easily in the saddle.

"Quiet night," Shiloh muttered. "Herd critters get skittish, uneasy, at midnight, though. Never knew why. Strikes me if —"

And suddenly all hell broke loose. Channing took automatic tight rein on his snorting horse, hardly believing his eyes. There had been a single shot — and a vast orange flare out in the night, then a sheet of leaping flames building itself magically into a wide, racing circle of unbroken fire. The whole tableau was highlighted as brightly as day. Etched against

117

high-tossed flames, heads and horns of cattle stirred above the massed black hulk of their bodies, not yet spooked. Spur and Mexican Bit nighthawks were trying, to bring their frightened horses under control. And now a second orange burst ignited at the opposite end of the herd, running along an unseen path to meet the other semicircle of flames, now widely surrounding the herd and riders. At the same time, a peppering of shots began from unseen riflemen beyond the fire.

Shiloh Dawes socked steel into his horse's ribs; it squealed and leaped forward with Shiloh's bull-chested roar: "Shag it, you buckos!"

They spurred as one into his lead, heading for a break in the wall of fire on their near side. Channing saw a squatted-down man rise from the grasses and start a panicked run from their path. A rider fired, the roar of his Colt lost in the merged crackle of flames, crash of shots, and cattle-bawling. The man stumbled and went down. Something bulky flung from his hand spurted a gurgling flow. It confirmed Channing's first thought . . . coal oil.

Somehow, as he'd half-guessed, the enemy had tolled in close to the outriders, disposing of them in silence. Then Anchor men stationed at pre-planned intervals had worked in silently with their cans of coal oil, sloshing down the dry grass of this waterless plateau in a ring around the herd. Darkness and herd-noises would have obscured their movements from the nighthawks. The signal to ignite the coal oil had been that shot. But it was premature, or one of the nighthawks had seen something in the night and had fired; the running man the Spur rider had shot hadn't had time to lay down his share.

This flashed through his mind as they pounded through the gap in the flames; a blistering wave of heat rode against their bodies and then they were inside. Shiloh bellowed: "Get on the other side, start 'em moving through this hole."

A rider yelled at the top of his lungs, "They'll stampede!"

"No help for it!"

Shiloh lunged his mount up the west flank of the herd, paralleling the rim of fire. The whitefaces were in full panic now, bawling and squealing; their aimless milling prevented a concerted bolt from the surrounding flames. Rifle fire from the invisible marksmen beyond the flames populated the night with steady, withering death; the heavy-bodied cattle at the edge of the herd were plunging to earth crippled or dying. The pile-up of downed steers would make a stampede still more difficult to begin. Yet every man hung behind Shiloh as they raced up the gamut of gunfire, picking up several nighthawks as they rode. Channing had already seen one nighthawk shot from his saddle, and now he heard a yell behind him and twisted in time to see a man spill headlong to the ground and crumple there unmoving.

But there was no stopping; it was ride, ride it out to the end where no hidden guns spoke, and Channing guessed that Santee's limited force was concentrated at opposite flanks. Shiloh's roared orders sent his men careening in a skirmish line across the drag. They

119

blasted the sky with their six-shooters, lashed at the rumps of the nearest beeves with their coiled ropes, screaming at the tops of voices hoarsened to husky whispers as a pungent reek of scorched sod scoured throats and lungs raw.

But the shorthorns were moving. Slowly at first, now with a ponderous shift of movement as the relentless push rippled through the mass to create leaders, and that fore-surge took the rest in its wake.

The gap in the fire-circle could not accommodate the bellowing, horn-tossing mass; those on the outer flank plunged back on their fellows or raced blindly through the flames which were not eating inward on dead clump-grass. A stench of singed hide mingled with oily billows of smoke. The rifle fire concentrated now on the drovers. Channing saw another man topple from his saddle, then stumble to his feet and stagger after his bolting horse. Then the shorthorns were galvanized into a surging juggernaut. The stampede had begun.

The riders raced after them, clearing the circle of flames at last, and the shooting fell off and was lost in their wake, and there was only the cutting wind against the face and the powerful surge of horse-muscles beneath. The sea of hurtling beef began to assume the form of a wide-strung crescent with a life of its own, racing down the last flats of the meadow toward the gash of volcanic rock that bordered its west slopes — toward a bloody fate unless its resistless momentum could be turned.

Channing was already spurring sideways toward the west tip of the crescent, the dark forms of unidentifiable riders following his lead. Channing reloaded his revolver with unthinking dexterity before he reached the tip of the flank. He fired, gunflame washing into the eyes of the nearest steers. Then Shiloh Dawes was recklessly crowding nearer still, rifle blazing again and again. The edge of the flank blunted and flattened back on itself like a rising wave, and the riders were firing, swinging ropes, hoarsely yelling like demons.

That side of the herd began to turn, and men relentlessly crowded it and guided it. A bunch split out from the main mass, continued its doomed rush toward the *malpais*. Another bunch followed, and another; but now the millwheel was firmly established. Through the long, dust-choked minutes that followed, the bulk of the herd followed a shrinking circle till the lead steers were eating the dust of the drag. Still the living wheel spun crazily and the men had to hold pace, keeping it bunched till from sheer exhaustion it lost momentum and the stragglers staggered to a stop.

Men drooped breathless and wordless in their saddles; horses heaved their sweating flanks, breath was released in whistling sighs. Channing shivered with the chill biting through his sweat-drenched clothes and lifted his bleary eyes, seeing the distant splash of oil-fed flame dying low against the darkness as it burned itself out. The grass was too sparse and short to sustain its artificial life . . . so the meadow was saved, and the bulk of the herd.

But men and cattle had died, and Channing thought of his own sinking, weary apathy and in it felt the shattered morale of the others. As though to punctuate his thought, a rider gasped: "I'm through! Thoroughgood can fight his goddamn fights without me!"

And a Mexican Bit man: "Either Straker pulls out of Spur's mixes or I pull out! We didn't hire to get burned and shot down . . ."

A rider a dozen paces from Channing sharply turned his horse and cantered forward. Channing made out the hulking shadow of Thoroughgood, who'd been on the first nighthawk shift. He was bent low in the saddle. His harsh whisper whiplashed across the rising mutters: "You yellow-gutted nits signed to this drive, you'll see it out. Then you can go to —"

His words trailed off. Without warning he canted sideways in his saddle and fell — limp and unconscious before he hit the ground; one foot still hung in the stirrup.

CHAPTER
TWELVE

Doc Willis, the bartender at JUDD'S — LIQUOR AND TOBACCO, yawned and hoisted his heavy girth from the creaking chair behind the bar to tug his watch from his rusty vest and consult it. "Fifteen to midnight," he said aloud. The yellow dog curled by a table lifted its head. It rumbled displeasure at the sound of his voice in the high, empty room. "Not to you," Doc said coldly. He rolled his three-month-old San Antonio newspaper and swiped at a fly buzzing around a liquor stain on the bar, half-heartedly because the fly was better company than that damned mutt.

Usually even of a week night you could expect a few hands from the outlying ranches. Sentinel was utterly dead tonight, with Spur and Mexican Bit herding up by the Strip and the smaller outfits, sensing something in the air, keeping close to home. Even the Anchor toughs, a drinking and gambling crowd, hadn't showed. Planning some mischief likely; Bob Thoroughgood had taken a tiger by the tail, bringing in that herd. Doc thought sourly, scrubbing with his bar rag at the liquor stain, that even trouble would be welcome to break this dead tension.

The rear door to the office opened a crack. "Doc . . . You can close up now," Anne LeCroix said.

"Yes'm."

The door closed, and Doc started to shed his apron. Cool woman, that Mrs. LeCroix . . . Likely working this late over her accounts because she couldn't sleep, but you couldn't read it in her expression or voice. Worried over that cold-hearted damn fool, Thoroughgood. Doc shook his head with the profound sigh of a man who had seen it all and could still never fathom the vagaries of humanity. He turned to hang up his apron, checked the motion as he heard the canter of a single horseman coming up the street from the south.

Occasionally at night a rancher or homesteader might ride in to rouse Dr. McGilway out for some family emergency. But this rider was coming without urgency, with almost deliberate unhaste. Doc heard him rein in and dismount before the saloon.

A moment later the man pushed through the swing doors and stood a moment ganglingly, awkwardly, blinking against the light. He stood a good five inches over six feet, wearing a white shirt with a string tie, black trousers with an open vest, a black coat slung over his arm. At first glance his long, homely face was apologetically mild, his thick hands were freckled and large-knuckled, like a plowman's. He might have been an itinerant preacher except for the gun thonged almost invisibly to his thigh in a black, fine-tooled holster. Then there was his jaw set like a trap, eyes flat and pale gray as a blank slate.

124

His boots struck echoes from the puncheon floor, crossing to the bar. "Mought I borry that rag, cousin?" His voice was gently underpitched, yet it grated like a rusty saw. *One of those Southern hill trash,* Doc thought deprecatingly, but his cue-ball head warmed with a film of perspiration.

The man bent and wiped his dusty boots to a shining black, afterward removed his flat-crowned Stetson and wiped the sweatband. "Thankee, cousin." He laid his hat on the bar and ranged his cold stare over the bottles behind the bar. His sun-faded red hair was long uncut, fantailing shaggily over his ears and collar. "Jis' a leetle finger o' that Kaintuck bourbon."

This one's well-paid, used to the best, Doc thought mechanically as he poured the drink. The stranger sipped delicately and set his glass down. His eyes nailed Doc's like lead bullet-heads. "Mought you say how a man gits to the Anchor Ranch, cousin?"

Just then the dog growled. Doc glanced at the brute in alarm. What the hell ailed him? He'd stretched to his feet and was trotting across to the stranger, hackles bristling. The man only glanced at him with sleepy disinterest.

The dog reached him — sniffed a boot. To Doc's amazement the animal flattened his lean belly against the floor and began to wag his hindquarters. His snarls trailed into a low, puppy-like whine.

Doc said softly, "You're the first he never tried to take a leg off of."

"That so?" murmured the stranger. He gave the dog a careless kick .and it yelped and sprang away, settled down a few paces off and laid its head on its paws, watching the man with eyes of love. The stranger cleared his throat rustily. "Ast you a question, cousin."

The office door opened and Anne LeCroix stepped out, her look questioning. "I heard that pet of yours, Doc. Something wrong?"

"No'm. Gent wants to know how to reach Anchor."

"Oh?" Her expression sharpened as she came across the room. "Perhaps I can help, sir. I'm Mrs. LeCroix."

"Brace Landers, mum." The man inclined his towering frame in a quaint, cold bow. "Be obleeged."

She nodded to Doc to refill Landers' glass, then said pleasantly, "I'm afraid there's nobody at Anchor. You see, Mr. Dyker — the owner — is up in the hills with his full crew, moving a new herd on his range. They may be several days, and you may have difficulty finding them. You are a stranger to the basin."

"Sure, mum." Landers toyed with his glass but did not drink. "Reckon the barkeep here knows his way around these parts?"

"Why —" Mrs. LeCroix began but the man cut her off with an ice-edged intonation. "Be obleeged he'd ride out and find Santee Dyker — and tell him Brace Landers'll be waitin' his pleasure at this saloon."

Doc's jaw dropped. "In the middle of the night?"

Landers just looked at him, saying nothing, and now the man's still, vicious arrogance pushed Doc beyond fear. He thought of the sawed-off Greener on a shelf under the bar; his fingers twitched.

126

"Doc was just going off duty," Anne LeCroix said quickly. "I'm sure he'll be glad to deliver your message to Mr. Dyker."

Doc looked at her, his mouth working in speechless anger. Anne shook her head, a single near-imperceptible movement.

Landers tossed down his drink. "Thankee, mum."

"A pleasure, Mr. Landers," Anne said easily. "You look like a man accustomed to having his way." With a nod at Doc, she turned and walked briskly back to the office. Doc followed, muttering under his breath. She closed the office door, shutting off the barroom. He turned wrathfully. "Miz LeCroix, I ain't no errand boy for a goddamn killer!"

"Keep your voice down!" she whispered with sharp urgency. "Listen, Doc. Get my mare at the livery . . . Ride for all you're worth and tell Bob Thoroughgood — about this Landers. There's no time to lose."

Doc stared at her owlishly from behind his thick spectacles. "Wondered why you told him that Santee Dyker ain't at his ranch. Ma'am, you're playing hellfire. This un's purely skunk-bit mean . . ."

"I know that," she said impatiently. "The whole look of him is killer. Santee sent for him for . . . a special reason."

"Like to gun Thoroughgood?" Doc said softly. With the observant but discreet inscrutability of a barman, he'd always avoided even a hint at her feeling.

Her eyes were steady. "That. This will give Bob time. He can come here with men, get the drop on Landers . . . something. I'll keep Landers here."

"Look," Doc said with difficulty. He cleared his throat. "Don't like leaving you with this fella. Don't know this range much, sure-hell can't find Spur camp in the dark."

"They should be near the Strip by tonight . . . about ten miles northwest of Spur. It'll be light enough in a couple of hours, till then you can hold to the road — then cut north to the camp." Her hand found his arm almost blindly. "Doc, please. Do it."

"Never said I wouldn't," Doc said gruffly. He turned to a side door that opened on the alley, glanced over his shoulder at her. "I'll ride like hell. You take care now."

CHAPTER
THIRTEEN

False dawn had begun to lighten the east to woolly gray as the riders paced into the camp on drag-footed mounts. The cook had left his big cowcamp coffee-boiler on the coals, and each man silently helped himself. They gulped the scalding brew as though to shock themselves from lethargy. Cookie himself was busy patching up wounds and setting several broken bones. The brief flurry of violence had exacted its cost in more than spirit; four men were dead, including one raider. Others were badly hurt. Yet Thoroughgood's vehement words before he'd fallen unconscious from his horse had had their sobering and shaming effect. Not a man had said another word about quitting.

Those not on herd duty had gone doggedly to work at hunting out the bunches that had stampeded into the razor-edged *malpais,* and for the next two hours the rattle of gunfire had pocked the night as they finished off crippled and hamstrung beeves: Channing and Shiloh Dawes had ridden back to the fire-gutted area for a cursory search which had turned up seven soot-blackened ten-gallon coal-oil tins discarded by the raiders, who had long ago melted into the darkness.

Now Channing stood by the fire, filling a tin cup and passing it to Shiloh. He poured a cupful for himself and set the pot on the coals, straightening to face the *segundo.* "It's light enough to ride him in."

Shiloh stroked his white steerhorns absently. His face was worn and drawn with worry. "Reckon. But damn — hate to move him. It's rough trail clear to the nearest road, and that's no easy grade. Could bring the doc here — but it'll take twice the time, and Bob can't stay here. Needs proper nursin' . . ."

Channing nodded soberly. The bullet had taken Thoroughgood under the heart, ranged between the short ribs and had not emerged. No vital organ had been touched so far as they could tell, but he had not regained consciousness; only a bull-like constitution had kept him in the saddle during those long grueling minutes of forcing the stampede into a mill.

Shiloh turned and walked slowly back to the linchpin wagon behind the chuckwagon, brought to pile the war-bags of the double crew. Thoroughgood lay in the wagon bed where they had left him. Cookie had washed the wound with whiskey and tied it up; he couldn't do more. They'd bundled the foreman to the chin with blankets against the chill. Shiloh bent over the wagon box where the linchpin's canvas top had been lifted back, peering intently at the pale, hawkish face.

John Straker came up, batting his dusty hat against his fringed *chaparejos.* He glanced at Thoroughgood. "Hasn't come to?"

Shiloh shook his head mutely.

130

"He's in a bad way," Straker said. "I were you, I'd waste no time getting him to town and McGilway."

"Maybe you'd do that," Shiloh said softly.

"Me?"

Shiloh humped his sagging shoulders. "A Spur man's got to see out the drive. Bob'd want that."

Straker tugged his mustache in faint embarrassment. "Well —"

"He's right."

The startled three of them turned to look at Thoroughgood. His eyes were open and lucid, his words surprisingly strong. "Be obliged if you'd see me to Sentinel, John. Your obligation's ended here."

"What're you saying?"

"Can't hold you to a bad bargain. You can't outguess the devil. I guess we expected everything but fire. We got it." Thoroughgood's first show of energy faded; his eyes closed wearily, voice shrinking to a whisper. "How many men, Shiloh?"

"Two of ours, one of Mexican Bit's," Shiloh muttered. "But they stuck, Bob. The rest stuck."

"No matter," Thoroughgood whispered. "That's three good men too many to lose. And I'm flat on my back. I can't ask you to stay in this fight, John. You may lose everything."

"But damn it, Bob! Spur will lose everything sure — and Miss Nilssen."

A wan smile touched Thoroughgood's lips; his eyes slitted briefly open to meet Channing's. "You say it. Will she stay in this fight?"

"You asking me?" Channing said guardedly.

131

"I got a feeling she opened up to you, you know her mind best. Speak out."

"She'll quit," Channing said unhesitatingly. "After she hears about tonight... three — four," he amended, remembering the Anchor man. "Four dead men. She'll quit, give Santee what he wants."

"Don't blame her any," Thoroughgood murmured almost inaudibly. "About ready to quit myself . . ."

"Bob!" There was no response to Shiloh's imperative whisper. Thoroughgood was breathing shallowly, but there was a husky rattle to it. Straker shook his head briskly. "Get him to town, Shiloh . . . fast. I'll stay with the herd, drive it to the Strip and scatter it. Least I can do. I'm no quitter."

A muscle knotted in Shiloh's jaw as he pulled worry-fevered eyes to Straker's. "I'll pass that," he said softly.

"Man, I'm sorry," the Mexican Bit owner said contritely. "I know there's more here than meets the eye. But you're half-sick worrying for him; seeing him safe to town's your job . . . Look, the hell with the bargain! I'm sticking because I want to."

"All right, John," Shiloh said quietly. He raised his voice to bring the Spur crew to attention, explaining the situation and that they were to take orders from Straker and his foreman Mel Daley. He gave two men orders to hitch the linchpin's team.

Channing had started to turn away and scarcely heard him; a sudden thought brought him to a halt in his tracks. The harried violence of the long night had dulled his mind, yet now the thought etched clearly,

132

and shocked him to alertness. An instant backwash of skepticism made him shake his head, but the notion came back in force and resolved him abruptly. He pivoted on his heel and went to his ground-tethered horse. The claybank was standing head-hung and jaded, and he threw off his gear and toted it out to the group of spare horses. He roped out a rangy lineback dun and started to cinch on his rig. Shiloh Dawes came up with his grizzly-roll of a walk and asked a sharp question.

Without turning as he adjusted the latigo, Channing said quietly, "They meant to wipe out the herd. Didn't. Know what that means?"

"Want to know what you damn well mean by riding out!"

Channing turned, one arm slung over his saddle swell. "They'll change tactics, hit hard and direct. Kristina Nilssen's alone at Spur."

"You thinking —" Shiloh began frowningly, but John Straker now sauntered up, coffee cup in hand, cutting him off smilingly. "That's nonsense, boy. You're thinking Miss Nilssen may be kidnapped and forced to sign over Spur and the Strip?"

"Santee Dyker's way. Was with Brock, anyway."

Shiloh said worriedly, tugging his mustache, "John, it might be."

"Rot. Even Santee wouldn't dare . . . *that*. We're a rough lot in this high country, law unto ourselves. But there's not a man in the basin outside Anchor that wouldn't join to tear Anchor down around Santee's ears if he harmed a woman."

"They might have planned it even before hitting the herd. Brock's an old man, they weren't about to stop at torture with him. And she won't browbeat easy, that girl."

"Lord God, that's true," Shiloh breathed. "They'd have to —"

"Only a notion," Straker said with a note of uncertainty.

Channing stepped up into the saddle, quartering the dun around as he looked down at them. "That's right. So I'll go alone. You watch the damned cattle, Mr. Straker."

A tug of reins turned the lineback's head south from camp and he squeezed it into a trot. Behind he heard the two men's strident lift of voices. As men did in a quandary, they might debate away the next fifteen minutes as to what should be done. Channing, with his independent way of incisive thought and action, wasn't waiting.

At a hard pace it would take him over an hour to achieve the Spur headquarters, and Santee had already had hours to make his move. Suppose it was a notion . . . logic could not shake cold conviction. He remembered the day in Judd's saloon, when he had seen Santee Dyker's ruthless ambition unmasked, and the man's self-avowed lack of scruple. By these old-time cattlemen's rough, stern code, to fight a fight by striking at a defenseless woman was illogical, but Santee would never cavil at means. In any case, he decided, Kristina's safety was nothing to take a chance on.

134

To conserve its strength Channing held the dun to a disciplined pace for a half hour. A thick ground mist had begun to cloud in swales and hollows, a milk-haze shroud through which upland trees reared like black jagged spires and great boulders were as sleeping cougars. The windless silence was eerie, sharpening the measured *clop* of his mount's hoofs.

He reined in to listen for a distinct sound caught briefly and lost again. Then it picked up once more a hundred yards off to his right. A single rider was passing in the paling murkiness, but he could make out nothing. About to hail the man, he changed his mind . . . no telling who might be riding this violence-shattered night. Though moving on, he regretted briefly his decision, realizing the unknown's direction was for the Spur camp, perhaps a bearer of some vital news. The thought lent fresh urgency to his certainty that Santee Dyker had only begun to fight. As the rough uplands melted away to the gentle contours of north Spur range, he let the horse out in a run . . .

In the clearer pre-dawn hours he rode at last into Spur. The main house was dark and still, squatting on its upper bench above the outbuildings. Overhead a storm was slowly building, angrily scudding dark clouds across the pearl-slated dawn. He went upslope to the house and swung stiffly to the ground. As he mounted the steps he had the wry thought: *More than likely you're going to look damned foolish in a minute, trying to explain this to her.* He hesitated, then hammered his fist on the door.

He waited before knocking again, then impatiently opened the door and went in. He moved across the parlor to grope down a murky corridor to Kristina's room. Sharp fear took him by the throat even in his half-expectation. The bedroom door was creaking ajar in a draft; the covers of the empty bed were mussed.

He realized he was shaking with a mingled complex of fear and hate, and he steadied down on it. *Don't go off half-cocked now; be sure.* He swiftly left the house and skirted the yard, searching the ground. There was recent sign of visitors, plenty of it in the soft dirt. The first fat drops of rain began as he crossed the yard at a run to reach his horse.

CHAPTER
FOURTEEN

"Mr. Dawes," Anne LeCroix said, her controlled words not quite masking a faint tremor, "will you sit down . . . please."

Shiloh was pacing Dr. McGilway's little waiting room like a caged bear, glaring unseeingly at some dirty lithographs on the wall. The building shook to a reverberating crash of thunder, rumbling off into the steady rattle of rain. He halted, turned to look at her. She was sitting in a sagging leather divan with a faded ducking jacket thrown over her shoulders, shivering a little. Her face was pale and drawn in the saffron lampglow as she kneaded a damp handkerchief between her palms.

"Yes'm," he muttered. The rusty springs of the divan launched a protesting creak as he settled down beside her. He hunched forward, his thick fingers laced together, looking at the floor. Again he retreated within his glum thoughts, unaware of the woman till she spoke again, and gently.

"I'm sorry. This isn't an easy time for you either."

Shiloh rubbed his chin absently. His fist grated over the stubble silvering his mastiff jaws. Finally he shook his head. "It's taking him a sight of time in there."

"The bullet has to come out. McGilway is a good man."

"He better be damn good," Shiloh said tonelessly. He sighed, letting his bulk slip loosely back against the cushions. "Bob was a heller in war . . . a born fighter any time. Outside that he's been mostly a close, cold-like sort. Ruth — his wife — she drew out the other side of him. Me too, once in a while," he added humbly, then with abrupt directness: "You'd be good for him."

"I want to be. I want to know him."

"Maybe you —" Shiloh broke off and got to his feet as Dr. McGilway, his slim, straight figure a little slumped, emerged quietly from the next room. His eyes blinked behind his steel-rimmed spectacles. He gave a jerky nod.

Shiloh released his breath, saying awkwardly to Anne, "I was saying — you'll maybe get the chance. He won't be doing much stomping for a while . . ."

"Can we — ?" she asked hesitantly. The doctor nodded, stepped aside to let them enter. Thoroughgood was stretched full length on a table, half-covered by a sheet. His upper body was bare, the flesh below his deeply weathered face and neck of a startling paleness — not as white as the bandages that girthed his great chest. His eyes were closed and his breathing was deep and regular.

"He's under ether," Dr. McGilway said tiredly, removing his spectacles and tucking them in his vest pocket. "It wasn't the wound as much as loss of blood. His clothes were soaked with it."

"He stuck in the saddle a good twenty minutes," Shiloh said pridefully. "Time to pump out a heap, wouldn't you say?"

Dr. McGilway gave a low whistle and nodded. "I'd say so. The man's a bull — and a damnably lucky one. That wagon ride here didn't do him any good either . . ."

Shiloh grunted soberly, eyeing the sleeping man with stern affection. It had been nip-and-tuck for sure . . . Long before the linchpin had reached Sentinel, Thoroughgood was out of his head with fever and pain, tossing wildly about in the wagon bed while the *segundo* was torn between the need for haste and his fear of hitting up the team to a fast pace. Before reaching the wagon road, he'd met Doc Willis, the bartender from Judd's, who had blurted out something which was unintelligible because Shiloh had paid no heed.

He'd snarled at Doc to turn his cayuse and make tracks back for Sentinel, tell Dr. McGilway to set up for removing a bullet. Dr. McGilway and Anne LeCroix were waiting as Shiloh had pulled up by the doctor's office and they had gotten Thoroughgood inside, limp and silent now.

Now, as his first overwhelming relief subsided, Shiloh thought of Doc and his gasped message. He frowned, casting back in his wind for its import. He turned to Anne. "Doc Willis started to tell me somethin' when we met. Must have been important, fat gent like him cutting leather that far from town in the small hours."

Anne was bending over Thoroughgood, tenderly adjusting the sheet that covered him. "Have you any heavier covers, doctor? It'll be chilly for hours . . ." She half turned to Shiloh, gently massaging one temple with her fingers and frowning slightly. "Oh. I'd forgotten . . . I sent Doc to tell Bob about that man. Guess it isn't so important now . . ."

"What man?"

"A stranger . . . named Landers. A bad one, gunman. He wore good clothes and he'd come a ways. Acted like he owned the place — insisted that Doc ride out and fetch Santee Dyker. Obvious that Santee had sent for him. I thought Bob ought to know right away . . . I took Doc aside and sent him on to your camp instead."

Shiloh's slow, methodical mind picked at it for a puzzled ten seconds. Santee had imported special talent. To Shiloh's loyally single-routed mind, that meant one thing: Santee was setting a deadfall for the man who spearheaded the opposition: Thoroughgood. Yes, it had to figure. No clumsy attempt, Santee wanted a sure thing. That Thoroughgood had already been laid low by a chance slug would not deter a professional killer. Shiloh's steerhorns twitched now with a grim smile. It might be for the best. A well Thoroughgood on his feet would stand no chance against this gunman in a face-down duel, Shiloh Dawes just might.

"He's still at your place?" Shiloh asked softly.

"When I left, yes. Doc Willis fetched me the back way, and I sent Doc home. If Landers knew that Doc was back without Santee, he might do — anything."

140

Shiloh gave a decisive tug to his hat brim, wheeled and stalked back to the anteroom. He picked up the Winchester he'd leaned against the wall.

"What are you going to do?"

Shiloh turned slowly, facing Anne in the doorway. "My guess, same as yours. He's here for Bob."

She moved quickly to him, her hand fastening on his wrist "You haven't seen him. He's evil — dangerous. He'll kill you without twitching an eyelash."

"Difference is," Shiloh said heavily, "I can handle this kicker better'n most can a six-gun."

"But you're no gunman! Someone else, someone who could face him on his own terms — Channing —"

"Leave it be, missus. You see to Bob." Shiloh pulled her hand firmly away and stepped from the office. He blinked against a vivid fork of lightning splayed whitely across the sky, etching starkly the buildings across the street. As the thin rumble of thunder began, he hesitated.

This face-to-face business was not at all like a soldier's duty in war. There were no personalities on a battle line, civil war or range war. A face-down was different. That difference was a cold-blooded sickness in some men, and in others . . . he remembered Channing's face after he'd downed Whitey DeVore. It was a thing that could tear a man apart.

So Shiloh groped in momentary hesitation. But Channing had ridden off to Spur on a probable wild-goose chase, for so Shiloh had convinced himself in his immediate anxiety to get Bob Thoroughgood to town without delay. *Anyway,* he reasoned with a spine-stiffening pride, *this is your job.* He owed Bob a life and more. Shiloh was not a complex man, and his thoughts swiftly refocused on the fierce loyalty to his friend that centered his life.

Resolutely he stepped off the walk, shoulders hunched against the steady pound of rain. He crossed the street, feeling the hard, cold reassurance of the Winchester against his palm and remembering how it'd been a strange matter of pride for him to master this weapon that other men used two-handed.

He shouldered through the batwings into Judd's, halted in the stifled atmosphere of stale liquor.

The man was sitting at a table in the otherwise deserted room, one arm flung over the back of his chair, his legs outstretched and negligently crossed. He gently set the shot glass he was holding on the table.

"Something, pappy?" he drawled torpidly.

The yellow dog was curled by his feet; it raised its head and showed its fangs at Shiloh. *His friend, one mean cur knows another,* Shiloh thought detachedly, hiking the rifle stock into his armpit, the barrel angling toward the floor.

"Yeah, something. I'm the man you want to see."

"Pappy, your name Dyker?"

"Not likely. You're here to kill a man."

Landers didn't stir a muscle. "You him?"

"No," Shiloh said gently. "His best friend."

"Ole One-wing," Landers murmured, "you're a sorry-lookin' ole bastard, sure enough, but in a second I'm like ter fergit your white hairs, dust your britches."

Shiloh's arm blurred in a movement that cocked the rifle of its lever-spun weight; in an unbroken movement he brought it level and fired. The bottle on the table by Landers' elbow exploded in a shower of glass and whiskey. Shiloh cocked the rifle again — waited. A bitter haze of burned powder stung the air.

Landers leisurely moved his arm from the table, brushed gently at the amber spots on his white shirt-front. "Pappy, you hadn't orter done that." He unwound like a rising cat, coming to his feet with an odd, loose-jointed grace. The dog was rumbling baleful hate at Shiloh. Landers gave it a sidelong kick that sent it slinking aside, never ceasing its hateful snarls.

CHAPTER
FIFTEEN

After leaving his horse tethered in a thick cottonwood grove on the south slope of the dipping vale where Anchor headquarters lay, Channing worked on foot down behind a big hayshed by the rambling maze of corrals. His yellow slicker blended neutrally with the drab, withered grass of the slope, and he took advantage of what scanty cover was afforded by bushes and boulders, though the slashing rain which dimmed the outlines of the buildings alone should have concealed his approach.

Darting in a crouching run, rifle in hand, he achieved the corner of the shed and peered at the shape of the main house through the rain. The curled brim of his low-jerked hat formed a trough that channeled down a stream of water ahead of his face, and he nudged the hat back, its slant then dribbling a chill runnel inside his collar and down his backbone. It shocked away the hot residue of clogging temper.

He sank onto his haunches, the rifle across his knees. Maybe it had been a fool's game coming here alone. His thoughts were a chaotic blur after realizing that Kristina had been taken. He had cut straightaway for the wagon road fork-off that led to Anchor, and short of his goal had made a circuitous swing-around that brought him up by the south. It was a grim reminder that he'd come to Anchor this roundabout way before, tracking Bee Withers. Yet even that time his intention had not approached the dogged, feral determination that drove him now.

With the hot edge of his wrath blunted a little, he could concede the thoughtlessness of this headlong pursuit of the abductors. But now, speculating coolly, he thought that after all it made sense. To have returned to the Spur camp for help would have consumed precious time. Then, mustering the Mexican Bit crews to a mass rescue could only trigger a bloody battle and add to Kristina's danger. This job was for a loner, which was how he thought and acted best.

Still, a sense of aching futility ground his teeth on edge. The storm which gave him cover had its liability; he had no way of telling how many men might be up in the house where Kristina must be, whether any lookouts were stationed at windows. He could have told much from the small sights and sounds of a clear day. The bunkhouse was shrouded in by the pouring storm and a single dim lamp burned in a window there — another in a front room of the main house. If anyone was watching they'd surely spot him if he crossed the open ground near the house.

He rubbed his slicker sleeve across his wet face, hunched his shoulders in a shrug. It was all chance and no choice. He'd make for the rear of the house and the kitchen entrance, let himself in that way. Moving in silence through the darkened rooms to the front, he might be able to surprise them with no risk to Kristina.

He came to his feet, lunged along the east flank of the corrals to the stables and carriage shed close by the house, edging down the foot-narrow alley between them. Ahead lay fifty feet of open yard. He left the mouth of the alley, running full-tilt across the yard, slipping and thrown off-stride by clay mud which balled his boot-soles. He reached a corner by the back porch, flattened against the wall as he edged up the steps and across the porch planking to the nearest window. The kitchen was dark; he made out nothing but a murky gleam of dirty pans heaped in a tub. He leaned his rifle against the wall, unbuttoned his slicker to ready his pistol for close quarters. Then he bent to remove his boots.

Palming up his gun, he moved, weight on his sock toes, to the door and noiselessly opened it. As he stepped into the kitchen and started to close the door, the knob was wrenched from his hand by a savage kick.

A gun muzzle was thrust against his ribs with a savage force that drew a pained grunt from him. But he was motionless; a slight trigger-pressure of a cocked gun was faster than any man's reflexes. The man who'd been behind the door gave a rasping chuckle as he warily reached to lift the gun from Channing's hand.

"We kep' a lookout, bucko. Case some lone fool came hell-roaring in like you. They's men in every room. You'd a been spotted from any side. Move ahead, bucko. Keep your hands out in sight."

Arms half-raised, Channing moved to the vicious prod in his side. Down a corridor leading off the kitchen, through a dining room where two gunnies lounged by the windows. They only glanced passingly at Channing and his guard; one made an obscene joshing comment which the guard returned. In the lighted parlor beyond an archway, the sound of low talk broke off at their approach.

Channing took in the front room at a glance, seeing the three men — Santee Dyker, his foreman, and his nephew — then seeing nobody but Kristina. She was small and straight-backed in a big armchair, her face deathly pale, matching the white fichu collar of her dark blue dress. A low, almost imploring "No" left her lips as she saw Channing. She half-rose and then sank back resignedly. Her shoulders slumped; he saw some of the courage that sustained her drain away hopelessly.

His guard pushed Channing to the center of the room, and now Channing took in the rest of its occupants. Streak Duryea, leaning against the wall, absently rubbed his cloth-slung arm. He met Channing's stare smilingly, murmuring, "Well, well." Ward Costello gripped the arms of his chair with whitened knuckles, nervous fear shuttling across his wooden features.

Santee Dyker, an elbow propped negligently on the mantel and facing Kristina, tossed his cigar in the cold fireplace and pushed away from it, saying dryly, "Stop shaking, Ward. Your prayers to whatever gods have been answered. Good work, Elam."

147

The chunky man who'd captured Channing said, "Want I should get back in the kitchen?"

Santee motioned at Streak, who slipped his gun from its holster with his left hand and trained it loosely on Channing, drawling, "All right, Elam."

The guard left. All of them looked at Santee who had come to stand behind Kristina's chair, his thin fingers softly tattooing its backrest. Channing felt warm sweat mingle with the raindrops on his face and trickle down his neck and chest, saying now, softly: "Didn't miss a trick, did you, Santee?"

"My dear fellow," Santee murmured, "that I enjoy a good gamble doesn't mean I don't believe in cutting the odds as low as possible — by whatever means."

"They hurt you?" Channing asked Kristina, and her lips formed, "Not yet."

"She's a fine, tough-minded girl," Santee observed. "She fought us all the way here — but showed no fear until Elam brought you in. Exactly what does that mean, Channing?"

"You tell me."

Santee smiled. "I won't bother. However, it may be a useful fact, one I'll bear in mind. Just now — how many men came with you?"

"Just me."

"Don't stall me." Santee's smile flattened; he made a slight threatening gesture at Kristina which she could not see.

Channing said huskily, "No stall. I came alone. I had an idea you might do something of the sort, came to Spur to find out."

148

"Without telling Thoroughgood or the others?"

"They didn't agree with me."

Santee nodded slowly. "Quite possibly. They're a simple pack, these basin dogs. Wouldn't believe that even *I* would harm a woman. I'm apt to do a sight worse, you know."

"I know," Channing said thinly.

"You do, don't you?" Santee said equably. "You have a rare habit of merciless honesty about people and life. So do I. No illusions. But it must be hellishly hard on a man with your scruples . . . Anyway, we'll take no chances." He raised his voice, ordering one of the gunnies in the next room to check the grounds, and the man tramped out.

Santee circled the chair to face Kristina. "Till now I've reasoned with you, Miss Nilssen, and very logically. A gesture doubtless wasted, since women are creatures of neither reason nor logic. However, I'll ask once more —"

"The answer is the same," Kristina said stonily, but it lacked conviction; she gave Channing a frightened glance.

"Yes," Santee said pleasantly, "which brings us back to that useful fact I mentioned. Follow me, Streak?"

"Channing?" Streak said gently, and when Santee nodded he moved away from the wall, jammed his gun hard in the small of Channing's back and cocked it. The metallic *snack* of the hammer made Kristina jerk erect.

"Have you ever watched a man — or even an animal — die with a torn spine, Miss Nilssen? To sever it clean

149

would mean instant death, but there are ways of placing a bullet that mean extreme agony or permanent paralysis for the victim." Santee delivered the words as coolly and precisely as a pathological lecture.

Kristina leaned forward, gripping the chair arms. "Stop it," she whispered. "I'll give you anything. But stop it."

"Don't stop it, Streak," Santee said conversationally. "As you are till Miss Nilssen has put her signature on certain papers." He walked briskly to a cabinet and rummaged in a drawer, producing several folded documents.

"This —" he tapped the topmost paper — "is the deed to Spur. One of my men experienced in such matters removed it from Lawyer Wainwright's safe last night. This other is a quitclaim for your lease on old Brock's Strip. And a bill of sale for your cattle. Other necessary papers to facilitate transferral of property, as drawn up by a shyster friend of mine. We'll bring Brock around later."

"You've gone too far," Channing said softly. "That won't stand up —"

"The odd thing is — it will, horseherd. A man bold and imaginative enough can circumvent any law. The average man will break obscure statutes and the like, but is restrained from large crimes by his social conscience — which is mostly fear of punishment. The ordinary criminal is too hampered by limitations of caution and narrow greed to make a big, clean sweep. Even your land-grabbing cattle baron is basically a simple frontier lout who understands only blind force

150

and a few clumsy extra-legal devices. Don't judge me by any of these; the big gamble is my forte, refined chicanery and judiciously applied force are my methods."

He's puffing his crop like a banty, Channing thought, yet he had to concede the truth, however one-sided, in Santee's cynical philosophy.

"See here —" Santee waved the papers — "Cholla, the county seat, is remote from our troubles. The authorities there will be ignorant of, even indifferent to, our little tableau here. Should the situation be referred to them, they'll be interested in nothing but the concreteness of these documents . . . as they'll be attested by a greasy-thumbed notary of my acquaintance."

"But signed under duress."

Santee merely smiled, dipped a quill pen in an inkwell in the cabinet drawer, and laid the papers on the arm of Kristina's chair. He extended the quill to Kristina; she automatically took it, painfully scrawling her name on each paper as Santee spread it out and placed his finger on the proper place.

Santee refolded the papers and tucked them in his coat pocket. He produced a cigar, carefully nipped the end with his gold cutter and lighted it. Against the bite of fragrant smoke, he squinted at Channing. "Yes . . . it would be awkward were both you and Miss Nilssen to swear she signed under duress. It might even hamstring *my* story, which will be that Miss Nilssen, sickened by the bloodshed, came to me and offered to sell out. Naturally I took advantage of the offer. I will say moreover that Miss Nilssen told me that she wished now only to get shed of this basin and everybody in it — a not unnatural woman's reaction under the circumstances — that rather than wait for the train she would ride to Cholla on horseback and there take the first train back to Minnesota. Thoroughgood is not likely to contest my story, though little matter; he can be taken care of precisely as Custis Thursday — as you two will be."

"That your idea too, Streak?" Channing asked quietly.

"Why, it was me beefed Thursday, bucko-boy. Didn't you guess that?"

Channing felt a cold sinking in his guts, though he'd known from the moment Kristina had agreed to sign that Santee could not afford to let either of them live. But he might at least save the Spur foreman . . . "You've done enough to Thoroughgood," he said quietly. "He caught a bullet last night."

Kristina gave a dismayed cry. Slowly Santee took the cigar from his mouth, studying Channing. "Dead?"

"Bad hurt. Shiloh Dawes was taking him in to the doctor when I left. He came to long enough to say he was ready to quit."

"*Quit!*"

Channing, surprised at Kristina's sharply objecting cry, said, "He thought you'd want to."

"Ah, now I've had my eyes opened," she murmured bitterly. "Mr. Dyker opened them. To worse than dying."

Santee gave her a speculative regard, saying musingly, "Strange words . . . your hatred of violence

152

was natural in a woman. Then — you're young, spirited, everything to live for, even with no cattle kingdom."

Her defiance was cold and stirring. "I've seen a lot of death, Mister Dyker. I have seen those dear to me kill and be killed. It made me afraid for a long time. Maybe, I think now, Kristina, you're selfish. It was for me I was afraid. I'm afraid still, very much. Only I think there will be no life worth living while things like you live. If I had a gun —"

"You'd shoot me? There's a little lady," Santee said dryly. "So Thoroughgood's lost the will to fight? Good, I'll ride to town presently and look in on him, show him these documents. They should be the final convincer, along with my story. And Lawyer Wainwright is a chicken-hearted old fool who can be scared into keeping his mouth shut about the stolen deed . . ."

"One thing," Channing said softly. "Just how is she supposed to have learned what happened last night to the herd, to her crew, before she came to you?"

"Why, you told her, horseherd," Santee chuckled. "You solved that detail by blundering in here. You left Spur camp last night to ride to Spur headquarters, worried about her. But you found her safe — my story — and told her everything. She came to see me, you accompanied her. When she announced her intention of leaving the basin, you said you'd ride with her, and I saw no more of either of you. I've already had her few belongings brought from Spur; they'll be burned. You see? You both simply — drop out of sight." A salvo of thunder trampled on the heel of his words, trembling the house.

"Bob will not believe you," Kristina said tonelessly. "He knows us, Channing and me. He will not believe any of this."

"I think he will," Santee said blandly. "Thoroughgood is well aware of your aversion to violence. Channing says he believes you want to sell out now, and I saw your violent reaction before him that day in Sentinel when I told you of our kidnapping of Brock. As for Channing's leaving with you — my dear, a blind fool could see the man's infatuated with you. Oh, Thoroughgood will believe me . . . though he'd be near helpless if he didn't. Badly wounded. Nothing to fight for."

Kristina stood slowly, her fists clenched at her sides. She did not try to hide her fear. It strengthened her defiance. "Yes, you think of everything, Mister Dyker. Except one. Justice."

"'A higher power than men's,' my dear?" Santee mocked. "You're snatching at straws in the wind. I'm a realist, and I'll take the chance." His tone became a brusque command. "Streak, get a couple of the men —"

"Santee." For the first time since Channing had entered the room, Costello had spoken. A heated eagerness flushed his sallow face. "Let me have them. Me and Bee."

Santee cocked an eyebrow. "You got brave of a sudden. You were shaking in your boots, minute ago."

154

Costello's flush deepened. "I have that much coming," he said sullenly. "Blowing his dirty —"

Santee cut him off disgustedly. "I've never doubted your ability to put a gun to an unarmed man's head — pull the trigger. That does take your kind of whiskey-guts, I suppose . . . Very well. Take Channing and the girl well away from the ranch. Find a cutbank to cave over the bodies, and it shouldn't take you long. The rain will wipe out any sign."

"We'll be back in no time," Costello grinned feverishly.

"I think not," Santee said gently. "No, Ward. Channing will be disposed of, and that's what you were waiting on. Afterward — you and your heel-dog keep riding. I don't want to find you here when I return from Sentinel."

CHAPTER
SIXTEEN

They rode the narrow trail single file where it followed the bank of a tortuous gully, formerly dry and now roiling foot-deep with silted water. Channing headed the file with Costello behind him and then Kristina, Bee Withers bringing up the rear. On one side the gully, on the other a low-rising slope mantled with shaggy pine. The rain had thinned off to a fine drizzle which grayed the landscape to spectral outlines a few yards beyond a man's face.

Channing shivered, feeling the cold damp to his bones despite his high-buttoned slicker. The dread of death had long ago been absorbed into his daily philosophy; the impact of its present certainty did not shake his outward composure. But for Kristina?

He'd hardly dared adroit to himself before now the simple goodness and far more with which she'd touched his life. There was a thing inevitable in the course of a man's life and a woman's that nothing on earth had a right to disrupt. It was this that shook Channing, and not the death every man must taste, the furious and hating knowledge that the best thing he'd ever know was ended before it had begun.

He lashed his mind for every possible way out; immediately, there was none. The pouring gully on one side and the timbered slope on the other blocked a sudden side-dash, even if his back hadn't been an easy target.

He looked over his shoulder at the three slow-pacing figures behind — Costello and Kristina muffled in glistening slickers, Withers' grease-fouled denims shedding rain nearly as well. Costello tilted the glinting revolver in his right hand, reining his horse with his left. His eyes were gleaming slits beneath a forward-tilted derby.

"No way out, Channing. How does it feel, death on your neck? You made me feel it. Dogging me across the territory." He laughed, a hysterical note in it. "Santee was damned near right — I was close to praying for a chance like this."

Channing looked ahead again. *No way out.* But Costello had Santee's absolute immorality without Santee's guile or guts; Costello was all bluster, using an advantage that his uncle had set up. You could expect Costello to make a mistake, and in his desperation Channing knew he must seize the first opportunity.

The land began to mount, and the downstream flow of the gully had subsided to a trickle as the party broke from the crowding timber into a broad swath of clearing. Costello ordered a halt, and Kristina and Bee drew up beside them.

Withers crossed his hands on the pommel and spat thinly over one shoulder. "She's flowin' light here,

Ward. Nice high banks, pull one down easy. Won't have to drag the carcasses far, just roll 'em down the side."

Costello nodded, taking his eyes off Channing for a flicking instant. "It'll do. Tell you what, Channing . . . I'll give you a running chance. Kick in your spurs, head for the far end of the clearing. An interesting spectacle for your lady friend, eh?"

Channing looked at Withers with his slack grin, at Costello's sadistic intensity; lastly at Kristina. She raised her head, and though she seemed pathetically lost in a man's oversize slicker he saw something flicker through the unspeaking resignation of her face. He met her eyes, saying nothing because these two men would soil it. Knowing that he had to take the chance now.

Or never.

He reined away from the others and slammed his spurs in. Halfway across the clearing an arm of dense young trees, averaging six feet in height, extended from the wall of forest. He veered hard toward the heavy growth, body drawn together against the expected bullet. He strained low in the saddle, knowing Costello would never let him reach the opposite wall of the clearing. In a moment he would be carried past the thicket's sanctuary; it must be exactly timed . . .

Now. He freed his right foot from the stirrup, cocked his leg up, and launched his body sideways as the gun thundered less than a foot past the outmost edge of the thicket. Body balled up and hands shielding his face, he lit squarely on the springy topcover. Branches and twigs gouged his body as he plunged through. For a moment a tangled network of lower branches broke his fall, but they gave way and he landed amid the close-set trunks, free of foliage at their bases.

He heard Costello's yell of rage. On hands and knees he squirmed between the trunks, working toward the deep shelter of the forest. There was a burst of gunfire, lashing the spot where he'd fallen, then a sound of running feet.

Channing lunged to his feet, bursting through the dripping undergrowth heedless of the noise. Three more shots, one whipping inches from his head. The underbrush abruptly gave way to a wide swath of springy needle floor beneath towering pines and he ran low and soundlessly, dived over a deadfall and lay hugging the mossy trunk.

He heard the footsteps slow, the approach cautious now. He raised his head enough to see Bee Withers, head ducked, flailing through the brush straight in his direction.

He flattened out again. His heart thudded against the dank earth. He listened, heard Withers pause, apparently to scan the woods, and then swing slightly toward the left. His steps receded. From where Channing lay he glimpsed the man's gaunt back vanishing deeper into the forest

With infinite care Channing stood and started back toward the clearing, calling on his tracker's lore and patience to approach without a shadow of sound. He could get away . . . but there was Kristina. And he had to get his hands on a gun.

He reached the clearing's edge, sank down behind a screening of leaves. Where the horses stood, Kristina still mounted, was Costello — gun in hand, staring fearfully about. Channing knelt and searched the loam for a pebble. He settled for a heavy, rotting pine-knot. He stood swiftly, hefting it in his palm as he waited for Costello to look away. Then he lobbed the knot in a high arc across the clearing with all the strength of his arm. It crashed in some bushes.

Costello made a bleating noise in his throat, whirling at the sound. He fired once. Then he advanced slowly. For a moment he paused, poking aside the thickets with his gun. He wallowed in, noisily beating his way.

Channing left cover and ran for the horses. Kristina gave a low cry, and he yelled, "Get back!" as he reached Withers' mare. The animal shied away and he leaped after it, yanking the saddle carbine from its boot. He swung around at the crashing of brush, levering the carbine; Withers had pounded into sight and was heading for him.

Withers began shooting wildly. Channing aimed from the hip as he turned, then, at the moment the rifle barrel hung steady and hip-braced, he shot. Withers folded at the middle. He clamped his arms across his belly, yet Channing knew he'd hit higher — a detached thought as he watched Withers twist in a graceless fall.

There was a rustle of soggy leaves where Costello had disappeared — and silence. Channing shot once, deliberately high. Costeilo's squeal was of abject fear, not pain. Channing was in pistol-range; Costello had the shelter, but abruptly he broke down and began to sob weakly like a weary child.

160

"Toss the gun out. First. You follow," Channing called.

"Yes, yes, don't shoot," Costello sobbed huskily. A pause, then the gun sailed from the bushes. Costello emerged, his hands raised, and slogged emptily across the sodden ground toward Channing. With the sharp draining of tension, Channing lowered the rifle.

At once Costello's arm blurred down; the Derringer cracked wickedly. The force of the near-quarter slug was weakened by the distance between them, but its hot, furrowing impact along his forearm numbed Channing's fingers on the rifle. *Damn fool, forgot that sleeve-rig!* The clear thought flailed against the blinding pain-flash.

He threw himself forward, and the hard slam of rising earth shocked his body to sentience. He heard Costello running, saw dimly his slicker skirts flapping. Awkwardly, frantically, he worked the carbine lever, bracing the stock against the ground as he swung up the barrel. The sights crossed Costello's body looming above; the gambler had to be close to make his remaining bullet certain.

The blasts of their weapons were almost one. Costello's gouged a muddy geyser; he jerked, seemed only to wobble in his run; actually he finished one pumping stride before he plunged down, skidding on his face in a puddle.

Channing lay a moment sucking in breath and hearing Kristina's voice but not her words. He did not have to look at Costello; he did not want to. He climbed to his feet and walked slowly over to Bee

Withers. Withers lay face up; rain laved his open eyes and mouth.

He turned to Kristina as she came running up, just looked at her till she said his name. He said: "It's done. No more butchering. You hear me?" He stopped, realizing he didn't know what he was saying.

"Yes — yes." She took his arm and peeled back the slicker. It was a scratch, but he said nothing as she tore a strip from her petticoat and tied it around his fore-arm.

Timidly she touched his cheek. "Do you feel all right?"

He tried to remember his father's accusing voice, and could not. This was right, there was the difference. He had done it for Kristina, not for revenge. The numbness slipped away as he looked at her. "All right . . ."

CHAPTER
SEVENTEEN

It was late afternoon when they rode into Sentinel. The rain had ceased, but the murky overcast had not lifted and early lamps burned in most windows. Kristina was exhausted, lurching slackly in the saddle as they rode stirrup to stirrup down the main street which was now a muddy channel wagon-rutted by long black pools catching yellow shimmers from the windows.

By the Stockman's Bar Channing pulled his horse around on a tight rein, seeing the five horses lined hip-shot at the crowded tie rail, all branded Anchor. Kristina followed his glance. "No, Channing."

"Santee's got those papers you signed. If he gets them to Cholla, into the county records, you stand to lose everything."

"No," she repeated.

"You said yourself, there's a time to fight." He almost added, *and a time to die.*

"Please, not you. There are five of them, you have no chance. Spur I can stand to lose. But no more!" He sat motionless till she said pleadingly, "Come along, we must see Bob. Come along now."

They rode on without words. Channing dismounted by the doctor's office opposite Judd's saloon and assisted Kristina down, helping her over the slippery mud to the steps. They went into the waiting room. It was deserted, but the door to the inner office was open, and they entered softly.

Anne LeCroix sat in a chair drawn up to the table where Thoroughgood lay. He was sleeping, breathing evenly, and Kristina released a breath of relief. Anne's head was bent; she was dozing lightly, but now she glanced swiftly up at them.

"Channing. Oh, I'm glad to see you!"

"Where's Shiloh?"

Anne swallowed, her eyes wavering from his. "The doctor's out on a house call," she said almost inaudibly. "I — suppose this is Miss Nilssen?"

"Miss Nilssen, Mrs. LeCroix," he said tersely. Kristina nodded to the older woman, her sober glance moving then to Channing's tense face. She looked again at Anne, levelly and almost sternly. "Mr. Dawes is gone? He did bring Bob in?"

Anne bent her face against her palm; sobs shook her. "Yes, he's gone! Gone, Miss Nilssen!" Her voice was choked and muffled. "He thought he had to defend Bob, I suppose — or your damned ranch —"

"What happened?" Channing laid his words down cold and hard.

Kristina moved compassionately to Anne, bent and put her arms around the woman. Channing's tone was gentled by the pathetic incongruity of a woman he'd thought of as worldly and hard-shelled being comforted by Kristina, a young and barely sophisticated girl with a hatred of violence. "What happened, Anne?"

164

He listened still-faced as she told of the stranger who had come into her place late last night, demanding that Doc Willis fetch Santee to him — how she had sent Doc after Thoroughgood. She had not recovered from the shock of seeing Bob in this condition when Shiloh, convinced that the stranger had been brought to assassinate Thoroughgood, had gone into the saloon to face him out.

"He wouldn't listen to me, these men don't listen to a woman," Anne said with deep bitterness. "I asked Dr. McGilway to try talking him out of it . . . but as we started across the street, we heard the shot." Her voice went small and lost and she absently patted Kristina's shoulder. "Well, it was too late. Though I expect we couldn't have stopped him, and certainly not that Landers. McGilway and I carried the body over here, it's in a back room. Didn't want Bob to see . . . in his condition . . ."

"Landers," Channing said under his breath. He remembered the name and the man. Prescott, nearly three years ago — a street shoot-out. A rustler named Ory Thomason, one of the Hashknife outfit, later said to have quarreled with Landers over a split-up of loot, had cut down on the Tennesseean from an alley. Channing had seen it — Thomason wildly emptying his gun at Landers' back while the tall man turned almost casually. Nobody had seen his gun come out, but Ory Thomason was dead before he hit the ground. Landers was of a breed hired to do the lone and big and dirty-secret jobs. A man with ice in his veins had an edge, no matter what his opponent's skill.

Anne was looking at him wide-eyed. "Don't think of it, Channing. He's like nothing you've ever seen."

"I was thinking of Santee," he answered evasively.

"Oh . . . yes. He rode up an hour or so ago. Wanted to see Bob, had something to show him, he said. I told him if he came in here I'd scratch his eyes out. He laughed, said he'd be back, and went on down the street — to the Stockman's, I guess. But he has four of his men."

"He's still there," Channing said grimly. "You told him about Landers?"

"No. I thought if their meeting were delayed — you or somebody might come before he was sent after Bob." She added, "But I won't ask you to face him; I have a gun in case he comes." From her lap she lifted a little pocket pistol, concealed in the folds of her skirt.

Channing was silent a thoughtful moment. Both Shiloh and Anne had assumed that Landers would be sent to gun Thoroughgood, a tragic assumption that had cost Shiloh Dawes his life. It could be that he, Channing, was the man for whom they'd brought a special killer, shortly after that fiasco with Brock at the line shack. Couple that with the fact that Santee would have wanted to be rid of Channing for his nephew's sake. The thought automatically led to another, crystallizing into the germ of an idea. Landers himself might not know the name of the man or men he'd come hundreds of miles to kill; he was not the type to care, a job was a job . . .

"Landers'll still be at your place?" he asked Anne.

"Oh, he's there, large as any tin god; he's taken it over. Waiting for Doc Willis to return with Santee. I'd told him Santee was camped back in the hills, it would take time to bring him in . . ."

Channing turned and walked slowly out to the waiting room, leaning his shoulder against the open outside doorway to stare bleakly across at the single rawboned nag hitched at Judd's tie rail. A foolish damned notion, probably unworkable. Still, if Landers had never met Santee face to face . . . like Santee himself — why not take a gamble?

He turned his head at Kristina's light footsteps; her contained face did not hide her worry. "I don't want you going across there!"

"Got an idea. See what you think of it."

She listened gravely till he'd finished and then said irrelevantly, "That Mrs. LeCroix — she loves Bob."

"Well, he'll be needing her now."

"Needing — who cares about his needs! Channing, I am trying . . . Do I have to say it?" As he started to speak, she turned away, pressing her hands to her temples. "A good girl is not to be shamed this way. You make me ashamed."

Almost roughly he turned her by the shoulders to face him. "Will you let a man say something — Kristina?"

CHAPTER
EIGHTEEN

He had not intended to say anything, yet having said it he felt a lightening in him as he crossed the muddy thoroughfare to Judd's. The other day he had left a barrier of harsh words between them, shaming Kristina's pride by withholding his feelings. Regretting now his too-harsh and uncompromising self-respect that had not let him retract those words, knowing since the moment he'd realized her danger last night that he wanted no life without her, he had left her with the glowing certainty that no matter what happened now, all would be well.

She's still a child in some ways, he thought with the ingrained pessimism of experience. He was tense-muscled, pushing through the batwings of Judd's. But the Spur crew had lost stomach for further fight, Thoroughgood was out of it . . . Shiloh Dawes was dead. It was up to him.

Brace Landers raised his shaggy head, his eyes blood-shot from sleeplessness as Channing came to the table and swung a chair out, straddling it, giving the snarling yellow cur only a glance before saying, quietly, "All right, Landers."

Landers' hand was arrested in mid-motion, reaching for a quarter-empty bottle. "Expected an older man."

"I'm not Santee Dyker. His man."

Landers' slaty stare was expressionless. "Took you a spell"

"Our camp's way back in the hills, took the barkeep a time to find us."

"How's Bee?"

Withers sent for him. Channing was on safe ground so far, with Withers out of the way. "Well. Sends his regards."

"Seen your face some'eres."

"Possible."

"Never fergit a face."

Channing tensed, seeing a dull glint of suspicion in the opaque eyes. Then realized that suspicion would be an automatic reflex with this man. "I was there time you downed Ory Thomason in Prescott. Didn't think you'd remember . . ."

"Never fergit a face. You wasn't with the wild bunch."

"Not then. Was mustanging under the Tonto Rim."

This seemed to satisfy Landers. Golden glints raced along his glass as he raised it to the light, squinting at it.

"Like to do my talkin' with Dyker, cousin," he said softly.

"No need, the man you're to kill is in the Stockman's Bar. I can point him out."

Landers set his glass down gently. "Deal was fer a thousand cash, five hundred advance, same after the job."

Think fast. Channing held his face to utter calm before the gunman's probing stare. Then he remembered the moneybelt strapped beneath his shirt, holding the proceeds from the abortive mustanging venture. "Right here," he said lazily. He tugged out his shirt, opened the belt and counted out five hundred of the seven hundred and fifty-odd dollars it contained.

Landers pocketed the greenbacks without looking at them, downed one drink, sleeved his mouth and stood up.

"You show me that there bar."

Channing led the way from Judd's with Landers stalking behind, the yellow dog trotting apace the gunman. Channing knew a cold and thorough hatred for the man which nullified his distaste for the savage deceit of the venture. He himself would have to face the guns of Santee's four hirelings the moment he set foot in the Stockman's. Landers, a strange face, would pass unrecognized. It was the only way.

As they pulled abreast of the Stockman's he turned to Landers. "Hold up. I'll have a look." He walked on to the big half-frosted window and looked into the smoke-hazed interior.

The Stockman's had a certain tawdry dignity with its mahogany bar and brass foot rail and a reclining nude done in oils on the back-bar wall. The room was fairly crowded with merchants and townsmen, doubtless because the bad weather had decimated business, and this was their customary port of pleasure while most of the cowboys and rougher element frequented Judd's. Santee Dyker was seated at a rear table, dealing faro to

170

three men in business suits, his eyes slightly squinted against wreathing smoke from his mouth-clamped Havana. Channing's eyes moved on, seeking Streak Duryea at the bar with three other men in range clothes.

Channing stepped back, almost colliding with Landers, who had moved silently up behind him. "How's it lay, cousin?"

Channing said low-voiced, "Your man's sitting at a table, left, rear of room, with three other men. He's about my size, thin, in his fifties. Graying blond hair, and he's wearing a light gray Stetson and a tan clawhammer coat." Channing paused deliberately. "He'll rile slow."

Landers slid out his horn-butted pistol, twirled the cylinder. "No law in this town, cuz?"

"No."

"Good, won't waste time choosin' him, no need for self-defense plea. Don't reckon no lily-innard counter-jumpers'll hinder me from ridin' out."

"That's your bet," Channing said softly. He moved back as Landers turned away, and when the batwings had swung to behind the man, he pivoted and went back down the street, walking fast. He felt no regret for Santee, a self-admitted murderer: only a strong revulsion for having to bring about his execution by this ugly deception. What Landers did not know was that the guns of Santee's four men would be turned on him the moment he fired. But if they didn't get him?

Channing reached the tie rail in front of Judd's. He tramped out into the muddy street and about-faced, watching the Stockman's twin doors. Landers had killed Shiloh. Sooner or later he would learn how Channing had duped him. It added to one thing: Landers had to be faced, and now. Channing slipped his gun from the holster.

From the Stockman's a shot hammered down the stillness. There was stunned silence, then a sustained outburst of gunfire.

The batwings sprang wide ahead of Landers coming out, his gangly frame crouch-bent with catlike grace as he pivoted smoothly and fired twice into the Stockman's barroom. Then he loped down the boardwalk toward his horse, the dog bounding behind.

Landers hauled up short on the walk under a porch awning. He was breathing hard; blood from a crease on his temple dyed his hair a deeper red and made a ragged trickle down his jaw.

His voice was deadly-gentle. "You didn't tell me he had gun-hangin' friends there, cousin." His gun dangled in his big fist at his side.

"You got handed some taffy, Brace," Channing murmured. "You just killed Santee Dyker. I'm the man. One you were supposed to gun."

Landers' breathing was a harsh sweep of sound. "You wasn't as smart as you thought, cousin," he whispered at last, and still he did not move, and Channing watched his face. When Channing saw the first break of decision, he started his move. He beat Landers' lift of arm by a fraction so that their shots did not quite merge. Landers' bloomed mud from the street as he buckled backward against the porch column. There was time for only fleeting astonishment to seize his face as he caught the second bullet. He rocked away from the column like a suddenly emptied grain sack and fell full length on the planking.

Channing sheathed his gun and took two steps forward. Then a bristling ball of yellow fury was streaking toward him, rising in a two-yard leap and slamming into his chest. Channing staggered, keeping his feet. He threw a forearm across his throat as the cur's fangs snapped for it. He felt the tearing pain in his arm simultaneously with the hot sear of a slug along his ribs. The dog's body jerked with the shot ripping squarely through it. Its falling weight carried Channing down to one knee before the jaws loosened on his arm.

A slug intended for Channing had killed the dog. His gun was already in hand, his eyes raking down the store fronts to the Stockman's. The man's hat rolled off with his sudden turn, exposing the bar of gleaming white in his hair as he quickly faded back through the batwings.

Channing sprinted down the street and lunged the swing doors with level gun.

And lowered it.

Brace Landers had done a full and bloody job of it. Santee was limply sprawled across the overturned table — beneath one trailing hand was a loose fan of cards. One of the Anchor men lay motionlessly twisted on the floor. Another was sitting down against the bar, whimpering incoherently as he held his belly. The chunky man whom Channing recognized was leaning against the bar gripping a bloody shoulder, and he turned pain-glazed eyes.

"No fight," he said huskily. "Nothin' to fight for. Santee dead . . ."

"Tell it to your friends at Anchor, Elam," Channing said flatly. "Then clear out of the basin, the lot of you. I just want Streak."

Elam's head tilted tiredly against his chest. "Back way," he whispered.

Channing straight-armed two gaping merchants roughly aside as he went down the long room to Santee's crumpled body. He found the sheaf of documents, pocketed them. Then he moved to the rear door, stepped aside as he carefully turned the knob and abruptly flung the door wide.

A gun roared in the yard behind the building, gnawing a long splinter from the doorjamb. Then there was a rush of running feet. Channing went out the door as Streak left the shelter of a pile of stacked lumber, vaulted a hedge and scuttled across the adjoining yard. He wheeled at the corner of the next building, got off another wild shot before vanishing streetward between the buildings.

Channing catfooted down the areaway between the Stockman's and the adjacent mercantile store, reaching the sidewalk simultaneously with Duryea.

"Streak!" He made the name high and taunting, stepping back within the areaway as Streak shot again, and again, wildly. Then Channing walked out, leathering his gun. Streak's fleeting grimace of triumph faded as his hammer fell on the loadless sixth chamber.

Channing walked straight for the Spur foreman. "Drop it, Streak . . ."

Streak lifted the clubbed gun — undecided. Then a gray courage sank across his lean face like a resigned shrug. He tossed the gun aside as he came on.

Channing sank under Streak's lunging straight-arm swing, brought his shoulder up into the man's midriff as he straightened, and the breath soughed from Streak's lungs. As Channing took a backward step, Streak bent with the pain, tried too late to rally. Channing hit him, driving him off the walk. Streak stumbled but kept his feet as Channing bored in relentlessly. A second blow arched Streak across the tie rail, bent at the waist. Channing whipped a down-chopping blow as though driving a nail with his fist against Streak's shelving jaw. The crosspole broke rottenly under Streak's weight and dumped him in the dirt. He lit on his shoulder, rolled over once and was still.

Breathing gustily, Channing swung to face the muttering merchants clustering the walk. "Where's that prairie-dog jail? It was Duryea ambushed Custis Thursday."

The talk ebbed into silence.

Channing said softly, "Santee and Anchor've made their last tracks. One more time. The last. Where's your jail?"

A pudgy man toying with his watch chain hesitantly cleared his throat. "The log shack other side of the livery."

Channing bent, caught Streak by the wrists and dragged him semi-erect, then stooped to let the limp form collapse across his shoulders. He straightened in

175

the same smooth motion and trudged to the jail. Nudging the heavy oak door open with his boot, he let Streak down on the floor. A wooden crossbar leaned against the wall. He closed the door, dropped the bar into its outside brackets with a hard, final slap of his palm. Holding kangaroo court on this one would be the sole pleasure of Spur people, them alone.

He turned down the street with the day's first thin shafts of sunlight topping the town's ramshackle outline washing against his tired and lid-narrowed eyes, and that was all, it was finished and it was ended, running into a many-figured blur in his mind, and there remained only Kristina. He forced his aching eyes wide and saw her, a small and proud-straight girl stumbling in her run down the mud-slick avenue, coming now to meet him.

About the Author

T. V. Olsen was born in Rhinelander, Wisconsin, where he lives to this day. "My childhood was unremarkable except for an inordinate preoccupation with Zane Grey and Edgar Rice Burroughs." He had originally planned to be a comic strip artist but the stories he came up with proved far more interesting to him, and compelling, than any desire to illustrate them. Having read such accomplished Western authors as Les Savage, Jr., Luke Short, and Elmore Leonard, he began writing his first Western novel while a junior in high school. He couldn't find a publisher for it until he rewrote it after graduating from college with a Bachelor's degree from the University of Wisconsin at Stevens Point in 1955 and sent it to an agent. It was accepted by Ace Books and was published in 1956 as *Haven of the Hunted*.

Olsen went on to become one of the most widely respected and widely read authors of Western fiction in the second half of the 20th Century. Even early works such as *High Lawless* and *Gunswift* are brilliantly plotted with involving characters and situations and a simple, powerfully evocative style. Olsen went on to write such important Western novels as *The Stalking Moon* and *Arrow in the Sun* which were made into classic Western films as well, the former starring Gregory Peck and the latter under the title *Soldier Blue* starring Candice Bergen. His novels have been translated into numerous European languages, including French, Spanish, Italian, Swedish, Serbo-Croatian, and Czech.

The second edition of *Twentieth Century Western Writers* concluded that "with the right press Olsen could command the position currently enjoyed by the late Louis L'Amour as America's most popular and foremost author of traditional Western novels." Any Olsen novel is guaranteed to combine drama and memorable characters with an authentic background of historical fact and an accurate portrayal of Western terrain.

ISIS publish a wide range of books in large print, from fiction to biography. Any suggestions for books you would like to see in large print or audio are always welcome. Please send to the Editorial Department at:

ISIS Publishing Limited
7 Centremead
Osney Mead
Oxford OX2 0ES

A full list of titles is available free of charge from:

Ulverscroft Large Print Books Limited

(UK)
The Green
Bradgate Road, Anstey
Leicester LE7 7FU
Tel: (0116) 236 4325

(Australia)
P.O. Box 314
St Leonards
NSW 1590
Tel: (02) 9436 2622

(USA)
P.O. Box 1230
West Seneca
N.Y. 14224-1230
Tel: (716) 674 4270

(Canada)
P.O. Box 80038
Burlington
Ontario L7L 6B1
Tel: (905) 637 8734

(New Zealand)
P.O. Box 456
Feilding
Tel: (06) 323 6828

Details of **ISIS** complete and unabridged audio books are also available from these offices. Alternatively, contact your local library for details of their collection of **ISIS** large print and unabridged audio books.